Look what people are saying about these talented authors...

Lori Wilde

"Wilde's clever combination of humor, sorrow and love brings a deeply appealing sense of realism."
—*Publishers Weekly*

"Lori Wilde pens a winner with terrific characters who feel like friends, chemistry, great sex scenes and a happily-ever-after."
—*RT Book Reviews*

Wendy Etherington

"Another winner from Etherington with great humor and unexpected characters."
—*RT Book Reviews* on *After Dark*

"Gavin is, as the title suggests, irresistible, and readers will be delighted with the antics of this Indiana Jones of the high seas."
—*RT Book Reviews* on *Irresistible Fortune*

Jillian Burns

"With *Let it Ride*, Jillian Burns has written a wonderfully steamy, fast-paced story that will keep you turning pages until the very end."
—*Kwips and Kritiques*

"Jillian Burns is an author who can take an ordinary, everyday story and make it her own. Burns fans will love this beautifully woven story and new readers will become lifelong fans!"
—*FreshFiction* on *Seduce and Rescue*

LORI WILDE

is a *New York Times* bestselling author and has written more than forty books. She's been nominated for a RITA® Award and four *RT Book Reviews* Reviewers' Choice Awards. Her books have been excerpted in *Cosmopolitan, Redbook* and *Quick & Simple.* Lori teaches writing online through Ed2go. She's also an R.N. trained in forensics and she volunteers at a women's shelter. Visit her website at www.loriwilde.com.

WENDY ETHERINGTON

was born and raised in the deep South—and she has the fried-chicken recipes and NASCAR ticket stubs to prove it. The author of more than twenty books, she writes full-time from her home in South Carolina, where she lives with her husband, two daughters and an energetic shih tzu named Cody. She can be reached via her website, www.wendyetherington.com.

JILLIAN BURNS

has always read romance, and spent her teens immersed in the worlds of Jane Eyre and Elizabeth Bennett. She lives in Texas with her husband of twenty years and their three active kids. Jillian likes to think her emotional nature— sometimes referred to as moodiness—has found the perfect outlet in writing stories filled with passion and romance. She believes romance novels have the power to change lives with their message of eternal love and hope. For more information on Jillian, check out www.julietburns.com.

Lori Wilde
Wendy Etherington
Jillian Burns

BY INVITATION ONLY

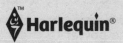

TORONTO NEW YORK LONDON
AMSTERDAM PARIS SYDNEY HAMBURG
STOCKHOLM ATHENS TOKYO MILAN MADRID
PRAGUE WARSAW BUDAPEST AUCKLAND

ISBN-13: 978-0-373-79625-0

BY INVITATION ONLY
Copyright © 2011 by Harlequin Books S.A.

The publisher acknowledges the copyright holders of the individual works as follows:

EXCLUSIVELY YOURS
Copyright © 2011 by Laurie Vanzura

PRIVATE PARTY
Copyright © 2011 by Etherington, Inc.

SECRET ENCOUNTER
Copyright © 2011 by Juliet L. Burns

Recycling programs for this product may not exist in your area.

CONTENTS

EXCLUSIVELY YOURS   7
Lori Wilde

PRIVATE PARTY   83
Wendy Etherington

SECRET ENCOUNTER   151
Jillian Burns

EXCLUSIVELY YOURS

Lori Wilde

To Debi Little. I so appreciate all your support.
Thanks for reading!

1

Breaking news from the blog, Man About Texas, by Nicolas Greer

Have you heard the word? Another good bachelor bites
the dust. Playboy extraordinaire, J. D. Maynard, (yes,
he is the son of James Dallas Maynard Sr., the richest
oil tycoon in Texas), went down on one knee in front
of Hollywood's latest "it" girl, überglam Holly Addison.
Rumor has it that Holly's said yes, and they're planning
a summer wedding. My heart is breaking, fellas. Say it
ain't so, J.D.! Holly's hot as a firecracker and all that, but
this is your freedom we're talking about here. Run for
the hills while you still can....

"YOU'VE GOT TO BE KIDDING ME." Olivia Carmichael crumpled
the printout of the odious Nicolas Greer's blog in one hand and
stared at her boss as if he'd just ordered her to strip off her clothes
and streak naked through Austin's state capitol building.

The managing editor of the *Austin Daily News*, Ross Gregson,
shook his head. Ross was a crusty holdout from journalism's
hard news heyday and she loved him for it. He was a visage of
her childhood filled with arguing reporters ringing the dinner
table and the television set perpetually tuned to CNN.

"Much as it pains me to say this, kiddo, 'fraid not." Ross was pushing seventy and sported a shock of stark white hair that sprouted straight up from his head in an old-fashioned crew cut. He always wore white dress shirts with the sleeves rolled up three turns so that the makeshift cuff hit him mid-elbow. At his neck lay a stained tie gone crooked from where he repeatedly tugged at the knot. He possessed a sandpaper-like voice, pugnacious nose and caterpillar eyebrows. He kept an unlit cigar permanently chomped in the left corner of his mouth and a foam cup of stale coffee on his desk.

"You want me to write like an uneducated frat boy high on Krispy Kreme doughnuts and late night reruns of *Harold and Kumar Go to White Castle?*"

Ross shifted the cigar to the other side of his mouth and held out both his palms low and wide. "Hey, I feel your pain, but the times are changing, and we either change with them or get ground under the wheels of progress."

"Platitudes from you, Ross? What's the world coming to?"

"The likes of Nick Greer."

"Ugh." She held the printout away from her as if it were soiled laundry. Out of all the bloggers in the world, why had Ross chosen this particular cretin for her to emulate? She'd had more than one run in with Greer, who was too handsome for his own good, and she had been less than impressed with his flip, in-your-face style. "I was born in the wrong generation."

"I hear ya, and I hate being the bearer of bad news, but you know the brass is all about the bottom line. It's a shark tank out there."

"It's bad enough I got pulled from cop shop to work on life-styles for crying out loud…."

Two months ago, the budget had been cut yet again, and while she should consider herself lucky to have a job, reporters had been shuffled and she'd lost the coveted police beat and landed in her own personal hell of fluff features. Her goal was to do so well in lifestyles that the upper echelon would realize they were wasting her talents on interviewing charity-ball-throwing socialites and put her back where she belonged amidst murder and mayhem.

She flexed her left wrist so the platinum bracelet she'd worn since college slipped down and flipped the Pulitzer medal charm—a replica of the one her grandfather's paper had won in 1946—into her palm. Her grandfather had had it made for her and had presented it to her at her college graduation. Olivia cupped her fingers around the charm, felt the warm weight of family obligations against her skin. She was a Carmichael after all; she had a tradition to uphold. Her ultimate goal was to be the best reporter at the *Austin Daily News* so that when her mother regained her health, she could return to D.C. and snag back her old job at the *Washington Post*.

"I know you're eager to make your mark," Ross said, his gaze going to her fist, "but the number of people following Nick Greer's blog outstrips our circulation numbers threefold. We've got to adapt or die off. Readers want instant news delivered in a flashy package."

"Journalistic integrity be damned?"

Ross shrugged. "I wish it wasn't so, but you can't fight reality."

"'Rage, rage against the dying of the light,'" she quoted Dylan Thomas.

"Gotta leave the battle up to you, kid," he said. "This old dinosaur is ready for retirement. But if you want to keep your job, you've gotta start writing snappy and sensational copy. Greer is your competition now. Not other print reporters."

She did not want to accept this. She'd cut her teeth on Walter Cronkite and William Randolph Hearst. Her favorite movie was *All the President's Men*. From early childhood she'd dreamed of becoming the next Judith Miller or Maureen Dowd.

Those hopes had taken a stumble when her mother had been diagnosed with stage 3 breast cancer, and she'd come home to Austin to help Dad take care of her. Mom was now steadily improving after months of chemo and radiation. And while Olivia had begun to think that maybe her dream wasn't totally dead, she couldn't deny the insidious virus that was the internet.

Nick Greer was a symbol of everything she disliked about jackhammer journalism. Just thinking about him sent a throb of disgust pulsing through her blood. One night at two in the morning when crime had taken her to a trendy nightclub in downtown Austin, she'd seen Greer strolling from the exit with two big-chested bimbos on his arms. He'd spotted her, grinned boldly and had the audacity to wink.

"Here's the deal," Ross said. "The brass is grumbling about another set of budget cuts—"

Olivia groaned and smacked a palm against her forehead.

He held up a hand, warding off more protests. "I'm just laying it on the line for you. If you want to keep your job—and I know you hate lifestyles, but it's better than the unemployment line—you need to knock 'em dead with this assignment."

"Which is?" Olivia held her breath, waiting for the other shoe to drop.

"Bag an exclusive with Holly Addison. She's arriving in Austin tomorrow for a brief stay before she and Maynard and the wedding party jet off to Rapture Island in the Caribbean."

"Seriously?"

"What can I say?" Ross looked hangdog.

Olivia rolled her eyes. This is what she'd been reduced to. Chasing celebrities. Asking breathless questions like, "So how did the proposal go down?" and "Don't you just love being an Oscar winner?" She shuddered and felt the urge to take a long, hot, soapy shower.

"My hands are tied."

While she might not be happy, in the long run, she wasn't a complainer. "All right," Olivia said, swallowing her pride. It tasted like a dirt sandwich. She pulled out her cell phone, switched to the notepad application and readied herself to type. "How do I contact her?"

Ross made a face. "We don't have a number. In fact, she's been refusing all interviews and she's hired a cadre of bodyguards."

Olivia groaned. "Ross, I'm not a tabloid journalist. I don't stalk people."

"No, but you're one helluva reporter and you always get your story."

Oh, he knew just how to get to her. Pump up her ego. "Flattery is the last resort of a desperate man," she accused.

"Name one person in print journalism who's not desperate."

"Touché," she muttered. "All right, I'll get this story, but under one condition."

Ross arched one fuzzy eyebrow. "I'm afraid to ask."

"If I get you the interview, you put me back on cop shop."

"First, you'll have to best the likes of Nicholas Greer and his ilk."

"You don't think I can do it?" Olivia notched up her chin.

"You get the interview, then I'll see if I can pull a few strings. If there's anything left to pull," he mumbled.

She knew it was the best he could do. The rest was up to her. She stuck out her palm. "Deal."

"WHATCHA GOT FOR ME, sweetheart?" Nick Greer winked at Wendy Stewart, the receptionist behind the granite counter at Austin's elite private airport. He deposited a box of expensive truffles on her desk. He knew Wendy had a serious weakness for premium chocolates, and he milked this particular pipeline for information on a monthly basis.

With a guilty expression on her face, Wendy snatched at the chocolates as if she feared he'd take them away from her and held the box pressed against her exceptional tits. "I'm so sorry, Nicky, I can't help."

"Did I mention these chocolates are imported from Switzerland?" He leaned in closer and cocked her his most woman-stunning grin.

"I've been sworn to secrecy." She pantomimed, locking her lips and tossing the pretend key over her shoulder.

"Ah, sugar." He lowered his voice, caressed her with his gaze. "C'mon, it's me. You know I won't tell a soul."

Okay, so he wasn't above a little flirtation to get what he wanted. No harm done. It was fun and he made Wendy smile. Yes, some people might say he was manipulative, but when everyone came out of a transaction feeling better about themselves, how could that be a bad thing?

"Really, I can't."

"You know, I've got two tickets to…" He hesitated for a fraction of a second, scrambling to think who she might long to see in concert, then swiftly supplied the name of the latest boy band slated to appear in town.

Wendy's eyes widened and she broke into a big grin. "Really?"

Now things were getting dicey, especially since he was going to have to score those tickets. He didn't want to lead her on. Not that Wendy wasn't sweet or attractive, because she was very cute in an Iowa corn-fed way. It's just that she was the sort of girl that a guy took home to meet his folks and Nick wasn't in the market for that kind of relationship. He walked a fine line. "Well…"

"Gotcha. While I can't say anything…" She got up and went to open the door of the small office behind her. From where he stood, he could see a large grease board mounted on the wall that listed the incoming flights for the following day.

"You're the greatest," he told her, noting that Holly Addison's plane was scheduled to arrive around noon.

Wendy giggled.

"I suppose there's no way I could get onto the airport grounds tomorrow?" he said.

"J. D. Maynard's hired his own team to supplement airport security."

That was a bummer. He knew all the airport security personnel on sight and remembered their favorite sports teams.

Them, he could charm. Private security? Not so much. "Right. Of course."

"Let's just hope an employee doesn't accidentally lose her access card to the back gate." Wendy pulled a plastic card from her pocket and pushed it across the desk toward him.

Transfixed, he stood there looking at the card as if it was the Holy Grail and he was Sir Lancelot. He laid his palm over the card.

Wendy settled her warm, eager hand on top of his. "Dinner before the concert?"

He had her on the hook. Since he was in for a penny, he might as well go for the pound. "You pick the restaurant."

"Le Veau?"

But of course she wanted the most expensive place in town. "Sure thing," he said recklessly.

Gaining access to J. D. Maynard before his wedding was going to cost both money and a sticky situation with Wendy. Nick just prayed that he could convince the wealthy playboy to grant him an interview, because Nick's next book contract hinged on it.

The blogging gig was all well and good—advertisers paid the bills, but his hope for real financial security lay in making his mark as a nonfiction writer. His first book, which some had dubbed the male version of *Sex and the City,* was a compilation of seven years' worth of dating blogs from the male point of view, Austin-style, complete with music reviews and celebrity sightings.

The first book had had a good run, but two years later, the royalties were drying up. Since the blog compilations had worn thin, he'd hit on a new idea for his second book. He'd pitched his publisher the concept of interviewing famous playboys who'd recently decided to take the matrimonial plunge. Secretly he couldn't fathom why celebrities who had it all were willing to exchange the footloose single life for the stricture of a gold band and list of "honey do's."

His publisher had liked the idea, but before they would

commit, he had to submit a proposal. To do that, he had to start somewhere and an interview with well-known glitterati playboy turned husband-to-be J. D. Maynard fit the bill.

"Wow," Wendy breathed. "Just wait until I tell my girlfriends I've got a date with the Man About Texas. Are you going to blog about our date?"

Sweat popped out on the back of Nick's neck. He could almost see Wendy booking the wedding chapel. This situation was stickier than he thought. Sticky, hell, he felt as if he'd stepped into a vat of superglue.

He held up the key card. "Um…some things should be kept private. We don't want you getting into trouble over this."

"Oh, yeah, right." Her hand was on his wrist and she was undressing him with her eyes. He felt like a Thanksgiving Day turkey.

Hey, you started it.

Nick knew he was at a crossroads. Wasn't his integrity worth more than a book contract? He paused. Thought about his dwindling bank account, thought about the expression on Wendy's face, which looked as if she was already naming their children. The sweat spread from his neck to his back, plastering his shirt against his spine.

But he dithered too long.

The moment for escape passed when Wendy took the card from his hand, slipped it into his breast pocket and whispered, "I can't wait for our date."

2

OLIVIA HAD BEEN CAMPED outside the private airport since she'd learned Holly Addison was expected to touch down in Austin sometime on Thursday to pick up J. D. Maynard Jr. before they jetted off to Rapture Island together for their weekend nuptials.

But clearly she wasn't the only one who'd done a bit of snooping. Journalists, bloggers and paparazzi, along with fans and Lookie Lous lined the airport fence. Heavy security patrolled the airport grounds. For hours, her mind had been racing as she tried to figure out how she could get past the guards and the other clamoring reporters.

Bupkis.

It was almost noon and she had nothing. She was just about to drive over to the coffee shop a mile down the road and get a refill on her monster-size cup of java when she spotted a sleek late-model red Corvette turn off the highway and take a side road leading to the airport. The car inched along, but didn't attempt to go up to the main gate as everyone else had done upon arrival. Instead, it turned down a side road and parked in the grass far on the opposite side of the airfield from the other vehicles.

Her reporter's antenna went up. Who was this?

As unobtrusively as she could, she broke away from the pack

and slipped behind one of the big metal hangers. When she was out of view of the throng, she stopped beside a large oak tree and peeked around for another look at the Corvette. A twelve-foot security fence circled the runway stretching between Olivia and the vehicle.

A man got out. He cast a glance both left and right.

Olivia pulled out a pair of opera glasses from her purse that she kept on hand for times like these and homed them in on the guy.

Nicholas Greer.

Olivia caught her breath. What she had not told Ross—why complicate things, right?—was that she knew Greer personally. Her best friend Mica had once dated him. He'd wined her, dined her and discarded her like a banana peel. And then he'd had the bad manners to blog about it. He hadn't named names, of course, but Olivia and Mica had known he was talking about her.

Mica hadn't been hurt about the breakup, but what had crushed her was the way Greer had portrayed her in the column—a spoiled, high-society party girl who worried too much about what she looked like instead of how she treated people.

Ha! That was like the pizza pan calling the petri dish shallow.

Olivia gritted her teeth. Yes, Mica could be a bit self-absorbed at times, but Olivia was loyal to the bone and she hated anyone who could treat her friend so cavalierly. Yes, okay, maybe she shouldn't have confronted him on Mica's behalf and told him off. He'd pretty much taken her rage with a wry grin. That damnable grin pushed all her buttons and he'd come off looking like a cool customer, while she'd been the nutcase thrown out of McGulicutty's Bar.

The memory of the moment washed over her as she watched him swagger toward a small side entrance where earlier a security guard had been posted. Where had the guard gone?

Better question, what was Greer up to?

A plane circled the airport and the now-distant crowd let out a collective whoop. Was it Holly Addison's plane? A glance over her shoulder told Olivia all eyes were on the plane. This was her chance. Quickly she skirted around to the side entrance that was wedged between two metal buildings.

Nick rounded the side of the building on the left just as she cornered from the right. Instantly Olivia dived into a choke of red-tipped photinia bushes for cover.

She cocked her head, held her breath, listened. Had he seen her?

Whistling. He was whistling.

What was he so happy about?

Scowling, Olivia risked peeping from the bushes, anxious to see just what the man was up to. He was so confident—the cocky bastard—that he didn't even look around to see if he was being watched. He took a key card from the front pocket of his shirt and swiped it through the electronic gizmo.

Presto, the wrought-iron gate slid open.

How had he gotten a key card?

Dumb question. The man could charm butter from a cow. Well, she wasn't going to let him best her. Immediately she started moving as swiftly and stealthily as she could, rushing the gate before it could slide closed behind him. She made it through with only inches to spare.

Just as the gate clanged shut, the airplane touched down. At the same moment, three helicopters appeared in the sky, hovering at the edge of the airport's boundaries. Paparazzi, she supposed, trying to get aerial photographs of the Oscar winner and her überrich fiancé.

Olivia felt at once triumphant and sleazy. Instinctively her fingers caressed the Pulitzer charm on her bracelet. She'd made it onto the airport grounds where the other reporters had not, but did that put her in the same bottom-feeding category as Nick Greer?

She didn't have much time to ponder the question because

Greer stopped and spun around, facing off with her like a six-gun cowboy.

They stared at each other. Nemeses.

The second their gazes met, a bullet of pure, unwanted sexual awareness shot through her, the same way it had when she'd had it out with him at McGulicutty's. She wouldn't admit it out loud, hated even acknowledging it to herself, but in a warped way, Greer turned her on.

"Carmichael," he spat out her name as if it was a dirty word.

"Greer," she countered in the same teeth-grinding tone of voice.

He narrowed his eyes. "What are you doing here?"

"Same as you. My job."

One eyebrow shot up on his forehead. "Chasing celebrities? My, how the mighty have fallen."

"Yeah, well…" She trailed off, unable to think of a smart comeback and angry with herself for her inability to quip on her feet. She needed time and a keyboard to devise rapier retorts.

"Tut, tut." He shook his head. "And you're breaking the law. Trespassing on private property."

Olivia stewed. Fisted her hands. Fumed. "No more so than you."

"Nuh-uh." He held up the key card. "I have legitimate access."

"My ass." She snorted. "I'd bet my grandfather's Pulitzer prize that your name and face are *not* on that card."

"You've always got to do that, don't you? Show off your pedigree. Well, you know what? It's your grandfather's Pulitzer, not yours."

Ouch. She squinted, deflecting the blow. "I'm no more of a fraud than you are."

"I never said you were a fraud." His voice softened.

"How'd you get the card?" she asked. "Steal it off the bureau of your latest sexual conquest?"

"You're still mad about what happened between me and your friend."

"She has a name."

"That was six months ago."

"Doesn't make you any less of a slimeball."

"You don't even know me, Carmichael, and yet you're so quick to make snap judgments. No objectivity. Do you think that maybe that could be the reason you don't have a Pulitzer of your own?" He nodded at her charm bracelet.

She would not rise to the bait. She had a job to do and she was not going to let this irritating man derail her from it, even though her hand itched to reach out and slap his smug face. She refused to give him the satisfaction.

"Or maybe it's because you're so elitist that you can't relate to the average working class Joe," he said.

Don't do it, don't do it. Calm, cool, in control. "You are the most egotistical, arrogant, self-serving son of a—"

"Honey! Is that you?" A woman's voice cut through Olivia's tirade.

In unison Olivia and Nick turned to see Holly Addison rushing across the tarmac toward them, arms outspread, a cadre of bodyguards hurrying to keep up.

"Honey!" the actress exclaimed again and wrapped Olivia in a bear hug.

Her mouth dropped open as Holly's exotic perfume enveloped her. Over Holly's shoulder she saw Nick looking simultaneously startled and bemused.

Olivia was so stunned that she couldn't speak.

"Finally, finally, let me get a good look at you." Holly stepped back and eyed Olivia.

The actress was twenty-seven but looked at least five years younger. She wore her natural blond hair—the same shade as Olivia's—in a thick sheaf that fell almost to her waist. Her eyes rivaled sapphires, sharp and blue and dazzling. She wore a simple pink-and-white wrap dress with a flirty hem that hit her midthigh, white sandals and diamond earrings. Olivia could see why people idolized her. Holly had a way of looking at you as if you were the only person in the world.

"I can't believe it's been twenty years. You look stupendous. And you've got the Addison cheekbones." Holly gestured with one hand at Olivia's face and touched her own high cheekbone with the other. "How was your flight?"

"Um…"

"Long, I know." Holly rolled her eyes. "Don't you just hate long trips? I've so been meaning to visit you, but my filming schedule has been brutal, brutal, brutal. But I can't complain about having work. Enough about me, what have you been up to?"

Olivia waved a helpless hand. Clearly Holly had mistaken her for a long-lost relative who apparently had been stuck with the god-awful name Honey. Olivia needed to set her straight before things got any worse than they already were, but the little devil on her shoulder whispered, *Why not just roll with it for a while, see if you can get her to agree to an interview.*

Holly turned to Nick. "And who is this handsome devil you've got with you?"

Nick didn't miss a beat. He stepped right up, extended his hand and said, "It's an honor to meet you Miss Addison. I'm Honey's fiancé, Nick."

If looks could kill, Olivia would have crucified him on the wall of the airplane hangar. She glared, but he wouldn't meet her eyes. The coward.

"Honey, you sly thing!" Holly exclaimed. The woman was as exuberant as a first grader on a field trip to Hershey, Pennsylvania. "Why didn't you tell me you were engaged?"

Without waiting for an answer—which was a good thing, since Olivia didn't have one—Holly hugged Nick with the same intensity. "You've got to be in the wedding party," she enthused. "I won't take no for an answer."

"He's got other plans," Olivia said, glowering darkly at Nick, who continued to evade her gaze.

"Nonsense," Holly said and slipped her arm through Nick's. "What's more important than escorting your fiancée to *my* wedding?"

"Absolutely nothing," Nick said.

"He's adorable, Honey, just adorable. Why have you been keeping him a secret?"

"Yeah, Honey," Nick asked, "how come you didn't tell Holly about me?"

"I didn't want to tell anyone about our engagement until I was sure you weren't going to back out on me." Olivia glowered at him again.

"Sweetheart," Nick said, "there's no reason to feel insecure." He lowered his voice and to Holly he whispered, "She's been stood up at the altar four times. She's terrified I'm going to do the same thing."

"Aww, Honey, that's so sad," Holly said. "No wonder you're gun-shy."

Olivia gritted her teeth. Things were spiraling out of control and Greer was painting her as an unlovable shrew. She had to put a stop to this mess right now. "Listen Holly, there's something I have to tell you. Obviously there's—"

"But," Nick interrupted, and moved away from Holly to throw an arm around Olivia's shoulder. He pulled her up tight against him. "I love her so much I'm going to prove to her that I'm sticking around no matter what."

"He's a gem, Honey, a pure gem," Holly enthused. "Now c'mon. J.D. will be here any minute and I know he's going to be thrilled to meet you both." She linked her arms through Nick's and Olivia's and escorted them toward her awaiting plane.

"Um…we're not going with you, are we?" Olivia asked. Dammit, why couldn't she think on her feet? This turn of events didn't give her enough time to evaluate what she was getting herself into.

"Of course. You're here. We're here. There's plenty of room on the plane. It's been twenty years since we've seen each other face-to-face, and I can't wait to catch up on everything. Where's your luggage?"

"That's just it, we don't have any." Anxiety twisted tight inside her and she grabbed at any excuse.

"Airline lost it," Nick supplied.

Olivia threw another eye dagger at him, but it just bounced off his glib hide.

"Oh, no worries," Holly said. "We're about the same size and I have plenty of extra clothes. You can borrow mine and I'm sure we can find something of J.D.'s for Nick to wear. We've got you covered."

THE FLIGHT TO RAPTURE ISLAND from Austin took four-and-a-half hours. Nick would have enjoyed himself immensely on J. D. Maynard's luxurious Gulfstream G450—in fact he made copious mental notes so he could adequately rhapsodize about the state-of-the-art airplane for his blog—if it hadn't been for Olivia Carmichael digging her fingernails into the flesh of his arm for the duration of the trip, and it wasn't because she was afraid of flying.

He knew the woman was punishing him for getting her into this situation, even as she smiled at Holly and simpered that she was a nervous flier and needed Nick to hold her hand.

He took the nail digging like a man, never letting on that he was the least bit uncomfortable. Once they were alone, he'd have a talk with her about her bad attitude. It wasn't as if she was completely innocent in all this. She could have blurted at any moment that this was a mistake. She might like to kid herself that she was better than the paparazzi they'd left back on the ground in Austin, but she wasn't. He took satisfaction in knowing that the Pulitzer Princess was as lowbrow as the rest of them.

Nick had dropped out of the University of Texas when the blog he'd started began to make a little extra cash, back in the day when blogging was new and cutting-edge. He'd taken off and never looked back. He had a talent for storytelling and people just naturally gravitated to him, women in particular.

His way with women had been shaped by his three older sisters. The truth was, he honestly enjoyed women, to the point where he was certain he could never settle on just one.

Well, he liked *most* women. The nail-digging, arm-gouging female at his side was an exception. Okay, yes, she was sexy even in that buttoned-up business suit. And he admired how she didn't use her feminine wiles to try to get what she wanted. He certainly didn't have that strength of character.

Which was ultimately why Olivia hated him.

He cringed thinking of the incident over her friend Mica. He'd been a shit. He knew it and he felt badly about it. But hell, he hadn't even slept with the woman.

Mica *had* backed off, but then the next thing he knew Warrior Woman here had shown up at McGulicutty's, reading him the riot act. As unexpected as her tirade had been, Nick couldn't help respecting her loyalty.

And the whole time Olivia had been chewing him out for his gadabout lifestyle—her words—he'd been wondering what her lips would taste like if he wrapped an arm around her waist, pulled her to his chest and kissed her silly.

Ever after, when he ran across her at media events, he had thought the same thing about those lips. Inappropriately, he wondered about it again.

They were sitting at the back of the plane, behind where the bride- and groom-to-be and their entourage lounged on dual couches facing each other. Nick and Olivia sat side by side on plush leather seats the color and texture of freshly creamed butter.

His gaze lingered along Olivia's tapered ankles to her lush thigh where the hem of her pencil-thin skirt had ridden up during the plane ride to reveal a sweet stretch of skin. Legs like a

Rockette. Slim, trim and as long as daylight during an Alaskan summer.

Olivia yanked at her skirt hem. "Cretin," she whispered savagely.

He chuckled.

"Neanderthal, caveman, sex junkie."

He raised both palms. "I was simply enjoying the gorgeous view."

"Knuckle-dragger, missing link, ignoranus."

"Ignoranus?" He quirked a smile.

"Part ignoramus, part asshole."

"I'll have to remember that one for my blog."

"Are you sure that it's not too subtle for *your* readers?"

"Don't get upset. My admiration of your legs is a compliment." He shouldn't tease, but damn, she made it too easy—all huffy and high-and-mighty. The woman was begging for a takedown.

"Oh, yes, what every woman dreams of. Being eye-groped by an overly hormonal, over-the-hill adolescent."

He laughed again. "I have to hand it to you, *Honey*. You *do* have a way with words."

At the sound of his laughter, Holly broke from her conversation, turned her head, smiled and stretched out long over the arm of the couch to touch Olivia's knee. "I'm so happy to see you so happy, Honey."

"Yeah, happy, that's me," Olivia said and forced a smile so fake Nick feared her face would crack. "Happy, happy, happy."

But Holly didn't pick up on her true sentiment. "We're almost there. We'll be landing in just a few minutes and there's a limo waiting to whisk us to the resort. We're going to have so much fun! Tonight's the bachelor and bachelorette parties, but you and Nick will have some alone time before then." Holly winked.

"Can't wait," Olivia muttered as if Holly had suggested she walk barefoot over glass shards, and she dug her fingernails into the flesh of Nick's inner arm one last time.

He got the message loud and clear. *Just wait until I get you alone, buster. You're going to pay for this and pay big.*

But for some strange reason, her unspoken threat just made him grin.

3

THE PRIVATE RESORT BOASTED long stretches of white sand beaches, brilliant blue ocean, numerous pools and cabanas—complete with good-looking cabana boys—three restaurants, twenty-four-hour room service, a spa, a sauna and a fitness facility. Olivia experienced a twinge of conscience over what she was doing—pretending to be Holly's long-lost friend or relative or whoever this "Honey" person was.

"Here you go, you two lovebirds," Holly said and pushed Olivia and Nick forward into one of the contemporary Caribbean-style bungalows that probably rented for upward of fifteen hundred dollars a night. "I'll see you at eight, Honey. Meet us where the limo left us off. I'll have my assistant drop by with some clothes for you guys to change into."

With that, Holly was gone, shutting the door behind her and leaving Olivia and Nick standing alone in the luxury hut where a single king-size four-poster bed with eight-hundred-thread-count Italian linens was situated in the middle of the room. A sliding glass door opened out onto an oceanside terrace.

"Dibs on the bed," Nick claimed and bounced flat-footed off the floor like an exuberant kangaroo and landed with his butt on the thick mattress. He rocked back on the plush pillows, elbows out, fingers laced, palms supporting the back of his head.

"Oh, no. No way. You got me into this. I'm getting the bed."

He looked mildly surprised. "Excuse me? *I* got *you* into this?"

"You're the one who said you were my fiancé."

"You could have set the record straight at anytime, but you didn't."

"Only because you didn't give me a chance. What was I supposed to do? Announce it in midair?"

He shook his head, clicked his tongue. "I wouldn't have taken you for one of those."

"One of what?" she snapped.

"One of those people who blames others for their mistakes."

That gave her pause. *Was* she blaming him? Olivia's cheeks burned. She was. "Look," she said, and pointed at the sliding glass door leading to the terrace. "Is that a naked woman strolling on the beach?"

"Where?" Nick vaulted off the bed, raced to the door for a peek.

Immediately Olivia claimed the bed he'd vacated. Admittedly it was not her most graceful ascent, but she hopped up on the mattress. The white-and-turquoise duvet was still warm from his body heat. "Sucker!"

"There's no naked lady walking the beach?" He turned back to her, his mouth pulled down in a sad pout.

"You are too easy, frat boy. Your rampant libido cost you a cushy sleeping arrangement," she gloated. "If you're nice, I'll let you make a pallet on the floor with the duvet. Otherwise, you can sleep on the terrace and watch the imaginary naked ladies saunter past."

"Oh, yeah?" A wicked gleam flicked in his eyes.

She notched up her chin defiantly. "Yeah."

"You forget I'm a rude frat boy," he said, and did some sauntering of his own, strolling across the room toward her, the glint in his eyes darkening the closer he got to the bed.

A ripple of apprehension rolled over Olivia. What had she done? She scooted up against the headboard, part of her wanting to flee the room, flee the island, flee the country. But the competitive part of her stayed rooted to the mattress, determined to hold the ground she'd conquered. And yet another part of her—the irritating part that was stupidly, physically attracted to the handsome troglodyte—wanted him to climb up on the bed with her.

Crap! He was calling her bluff.

He crawled up the bed, first one knee on the mattress, then the other, coming straight toward her, a lion on the hunt.

Olivia dived, trying to roll off the bed, but Nick was quicker. He leaped, pinning her to the mattress.

"Get off of me, you oaf." She grunted, pushing against his chest with both hands, but she couldn't budge him. He was much stronger than he looked, but oddly instead of feeling threatened, she felt strangely…*protected*. How could that be? Maybe it was the bone-deep humor in his gaze.

"Who's the sucker now?" he teased, his voice a sweet caress.

She stopped struggling. Moving was only revving up the attraction. Contact with his sinewy biceps and muscular pecs sent hot wisps of steam smoking through her veins.

"Well?" he drawled. "No smart-mouthed comeback?"

None. Her mind was numb and she wasn't a quipper in the best of circumstances. But this went beyond that. It was as if he'd kidnapped her brain and was holding it for ransom.

His breath was warm on her face. He smelled good. Too good. Why was her pulse jumping? Why was her heart thudding? The man was a playboy. She knew that about him. He stood for everything she disliked—slipshod journalism; lack of fidelity; unbridled, exuberant goofiness.

And yet here she was, practically lying underneath him, staring into eyes that she'd initially thought were brown, but upon closer examination proved to be an intoxicating blend of milk chocolate and gold, and she was wishing he would kiss her until she couldn't breathe. Oh, yes, she was.

Don't forget, not for one minute, that he's a libertine of the highest order.

Then she felt his erection straining through his slacks, pressing into her upper thigh. She closed her eyes, licked her lips. The man wanted her.

Big deal. He probably wants any available female from age twenty-one to sixty.

All at once, the teasing drained from his face and he looked… well, like she felt.

Ambushed.

He was poised over her, hard as salami and she was staring into his eyes and the bed was soft beneath them and they were breathing in tandem, alone on an island, pretending to be engaged. It was a heady, intoxicating formula for sheer disaster.

Thankfully a knock sounded on the door. They sprang apart. Nick shooting left, Olivia darting right, both flustered.

Nick turned his back to her, ducked his head and slapped a palm against the nape of his neck. Olivia smoothed down her pin-striped business skirt, ran fingers through her mussed hair, cleared her throat and moved to open the door.

A young woman with a shy smile stood in the hallway, her arms piled high with clothing. "From Miss Carmichael and Mr. Maynard," she said, and deposited the clothes in Olivia's arms.

"Thank you," she said.

The woman stood there expectantly. Oh, yes, she wanted a tip.

"Greer," Olivia called over her shoulder. "You got a couple of bucks?"

He trotted over, peeling a twenty from his pocket. Was he was one of those show-offs who overtipped to prove how cool he was? More than likely he was priming a potential conquest. Nick handed the bill to the woman with a wink and a smile.

As expected, the young woman melted, simpering, "Thank you, thank you."

Nick closed the door behind her.

Olivia rolled her eyes and dumped the clothes on the bed, now rumpled from where they'd lain on it. "Was there ever a time in your life when women didn't fall all over you?"

"Nope," he said easily and raked a hot gaze down her body.

Heightened awareness blasted through her and she curled her fingers into fists. She shivered and hated herself for her reaction to him. She was *not* going to be like every other woman on the planet who seemed to think this man hung the moon and the stars. "You don't feel the least bit remorseful about it, do you?"

"Why should I feel remorseful because women like me?"

"You take advantage of the attraction."

"No more than they take advantage of me."

She groaned. "Not all women like you."

"Meaning *you* don't like me."

"Yes. I don't like you."

He shrugged as if it didn't matter one whit whether she did or not. "You gonna change?"

She startled. "Change? Why should I change? I'm not suddenly going to lower my standards just because I'm forced to be in your company. I—"

"I meant your clothes," he interrupted. "That business suit looks pretty uncomfortable."

"Oh." Embarrassment scorched her cheeks. "Well, yes, I am going to change." She snatched up the first outfit she grabbed—a skirt and T-shirt on a hanger—and hustled into the adjoining bathroom.

She locked the door closed behind her. The bathroom was just as lavish as the bedroom. White marble floor, gold fixtures, a massive spa tub with heated jets. She pressed her forehead against the wall, felt the cool tile against her feverish skin. What was she doing here? How had she let this happen?

Job.

Oh, yes, her job. She'd lied about her identity in order to get an exclusive with Holly Carmichael. And she'd somehow wound up sharing a quaint bungalow with the last man on the earth she wanted to share a sexy island getaway with—her archrival.

And yet, she couldn't deny the spark between them. What was wrong with her that she secretly liked the man she outwardly despised?

NICK PACED THE BEDROOM. Blowing out his breath, he jammed his fingers through his hair. *Okay, okay, she's just a woman like any other.*

But even as he thought it, he felt something completely different. Something he'd never quite felt before when it came to women.

Fear.

He was afraid of Olivia Carmichael and he couldn't really say why.

His mind wandered back to the stupid stunt he'd pulled, climbing up on the bed beside her, trying to rattle her. Instead, he'd been the one shaken to the core. She'd turned up her nose at his moves, contemptuous, not falling for his charmer shtick.

Did he want her merely because she didn't want him?

He almost bolted. Almost left the room before she came back. Dust in the wind. But he stayed, clearly a glutton for punishment.

Olivia came stalking from the bathroom, a look of grim determination on her face. He expected another battle over the bed, but one look at her and his mind went blank of all thoughts except one.

Sex.

Hot, sticky sex.

Long, slow sex. Wet sex. Playful sex. Angry sex. Make-up sex. Any damn kind of sex with *this* woman.

She wore a sleeveless red T-shirt that molded over her breasts as though it was spray-painted on and a white flared skirt so short he would have been able to see her panties if she bent over.

His tongue plaited into a pretzel and he wheezed in a chuff of air, but she didn't even notice. Her head was down, her gaze fixed on the purse she'd dropped on the floor beside the door when they'd come into the room. She barreled straight for it.

A normal person would have taken the purposeful walk and concentrated his expression on her face as a clue and stepped the hell out of the way, but Nick's brain had short-circuited the second she stepped from the bathroom. He just stood there, watching her come at him, his arms akimbo, his mouth stupidly hanging open as if he'd never seen a beautiful woman hell-bent on a mission before.

She clocked him with her shoulder, slamming into his extended arm, spinning him halfway around like the north wind on a weather vane, knocking him off balance. He stumbled against the coffee table and reflexively reached out to grab hold of something to stay on his feet.

What he ended up grabbing was Olivia. Her breast to be precise. It was completely accidental, but he knew she wouldn't believe that. She gasped and swung her arm up, trying to shove him away from her,

But it was too late. They were going down together.

He fell onto his back on the jute rug covering the hardwood floor with Olivia on top of him, her breasts squashed against his chest. He stared up at her. She blinked down at him. His hands had a mind of their own as they slipped around her waist, pulled her closer. Even as he did it, he knew it was a face-slapping offense.

"This is low, Greer, even for you." She stuck with glowering instead of violence. She would have been within her rights to smack his cheek, but she didn't. Why?

"Hey, you were the one who ran into me."

"You should have moved. If you hadn't stood there ogling me you could have moved."

"Honey." He chuckled. "The way you look in that outfit no man could have moved."

Her cheeks colored. "You're incorrigible."

"You're the bulldozer and yet I'm the bad guy? No wonder you're not in a relationship."

"Who says I'm not in a relationship?"

"Are you?"

"No," she said hotly, then muttered a curse and pushed up, breaking the light grip he had on her waist and scrambling to her feet.

"Who was he?" Nick asked, sitting up.

"Who was who?" She dusted herself off as if she'd gotten dirty simply by touching him.

"The guy who soured you on men."

"Not all men," she said. "Just men like you."

"Men like me?"

"Arrogant, egotistical."

"What was his name?"

"That's none of your business."

"So there was a guy." Nick snapped his fingers. "I knew it. What did he do?"

"Nothing you haven't done to hundreds of women."

He felt her pain like a kick to the gut. Someone *had* hurt her, and his impulse was to hunt the guy down and kick his butt the same way he would if any guy hurt one of his sisters. But there was an added dimension to this feeling that was far from brotherly, and that disturbed him. "Now you're just trying to hurt my feelings."

"He was an irascible rake just like you."

"Rake? Who are you? Jane Austen?"

"It's a perfectly good word and fits you to a tee—charming, handsome but bad to the bone. Cavalierly tossing women away like used tissues."

"You think I'm handsome?" Feeling ridiculously pleased, Nick ambled to his feet.

Olivia snorted indelicately. "Get over yourself already. There's more to being a man than possessing a pretty face and killer body."

"You think I have a killer body?"

"For crying out loud!" She threw her hands into the air. "Ego, ego, ego."

"Yeah, like *you* don't have an ego."

"Not like yours."

"You've got Pulitzer dreams, Honey. It takes a big ego to pull that off."

"Don't call me that."

"Hey, we're undercover. Honey is the name you got stuck with, although…" He angled his head, studied her. "It fits. You've got that golden complexion, a bee stinger for a tongue and those sweet…" He dropped his gaze to her breasts.

"Shut up."

He came across the room toward her. She was busy digging around in her purse and pointedly trying to ignore him.

"I like this undercover thing," he said.

"You would."

"Getting down and dirty, unearthing dark secrets. I'll be Deep Throat. You can be Woodward and Bernstein."

"Why am I two people?" She took a tablet computer and electrical cord from her purse and looked around for a place to plug it in.

"It takes both of those reporters to make one of you."

A pleased smile flitted across her lips.

"Ha!" He pointed at her sly mouth. "Gotcha. You *do* think you're as good as Woodward and Bernstein put together."

Her smile disappeared. "Bite me."

"Oh-ho, you can dish it, but you can't take it."

"Stop coming on to me. You broke my best friend's heart."

"I didn't break Mica's heart. We only went on three dates. I never even slept with her."

That shut her up. Olivia eyes widened and she stared at him

for a long moment and then finally echoed, "You never slept with her?"

"You thought I did?"

Olivia sniffed. "I assumed you sleep with everyone you date."

"And we both know what they say about people who *ass-u-me*."

"Is everything a joke with you?" She found the electrical socket and leaned over to plug in her computer.

Nick inclined his head. His gaze glued to her every movement as he hoped for a glimpse of those delectable upper thighs hiding beneath the flirty skirt hem.

"Mmm, not everything."

She straightened, spun around, caught him staring at her rump and immediately flattened her palm against the back of her skirt. "You are a rascal."

"Yeah," he agreed, grinning. "Rascally rake, that's me."

She glared. He was getting a lot of those from her. "Can you find somewhere else to be?"

"You writing?"

"Researching."

"What?"

"Who."

"Huh?"

Olivia plunked down at the rattan desk, powered on her tablet. "I'm researching a person. More precisely, this Honey person."

"On the internet?"

"No, on my crystal ball."

"Ha! I knew it. You really are a witch."

"And you're a jackass."

He winced. "That insult isn't up to your caliber. I've got a knife sharpener on my key chain if your tongue's getting dull. Wanna borrow it?"

"Seriously, could you just go? I work better in silence." Frowning, she pretended to focus on her computer screen, but he could tell from the rigid way she was holding her shoulders that she was very aware of him.

"There are better ways of finding out who Honey is without cloistering yourself in a room when there's a beautiful beach beckoning."

"Alliteration, the cheapest figure of speech. Why am I not surprised it's your fallback position?"

"Ah, there it is. You got your barb back."

"Are you always this annoying?"

"Betcha I can find out more about Honey in five minutes than you can in a hour searching the web."

She jerked her head up, a wicked gleam in her eyes. "You're on."

Ah, so competition was what revved Ms. Carmichael's engines. He should have known. She was the overachieving, only child of an affluent family. It was pretty well a given. Yes, he'd looked her up on Google after she lit into him over Mica. She'd piqued his curiosity. He'd discovered she'd gone to the right schools, dated the right men, did exactly what Mommy and Daddy expected of her and did it better than most anyone else. No wonder she was so uptight, sitting there kneading her neck muscles.

Damn, his fingers itched to knead them for her.

"So what are we betting?" she asked.

"Meet me back here in an hour. We'll compare notes. Whoever has the most intel on Honey wins."

"Wins what?"

Olivia tossed a gaze at the bed, and for one glorious minute he thought she was going to tell him he'd get one night of pure sexual pleasure with her. His cock got harder.

"Winner takes the bed, loser has to sleep on the terrace chaise lounge," she proposed.

"We could share the bed," he teased, mostly out of habit. He'd known bedding her was a long shot.

"In your dreams and my nightmares."

"Hands to myself, I promise." He raised his palms.

"Do I look like a complete idiot?"

"Not at all."

"If you want to take the bet, that's as good as my offer is going to get. You win, you get the bed. You lose, it's the chaise. Take it or leave it."

"I'll take it," he said hastily, even as disappointment tasted like day-old mutton on the back of his tongue.

Why was he so disappointed? He'd been shot down before. Granted not a lot, but it had happened and when it did, the rejections had rolled right off his back and he'd happily moved on to a more willing woman. Life was too short to waste time with someone who wasn't interested.

Except suddenly, the philosophy that had dominated his love life seemed short-sighted. What if she really was interested, but just didn't want to be? Maybe if he pushed a little he could knock down some of her resistance.

"Honey," he said. "You've got yourself a bet."

4

THE SECOND NICK LEFT the bungalow, Olivia heaved out a long-held sigh. She was alarmed to discover her hand was trembling. To stop it she sat on her hands.

Okay, calm down. Do some yoga breathing.

She'd taken yoga for years and it never failed to calm her down, but this time it didn't work. She tried to concentrate and search the web, but feeling restless, she flipped off her computer after a few minutes, got to her feet and decided to take a walk on the beach. Never mind that she was going to lose her bet with Nick. The chaise looked comfortable enough, even though it grated against her competitive nature to throw in the towel.

She kicked off her shoes, slid open the glass door and stepped out onto the warm sand. The sound of the lulling ocean calmed her. She started out across the beach when she spied Nick swinging in a hammock just a few feet from the bungalow. His eyes were closed, his hands clasped together over his chest. Beside him hung an empty hammock.

Olivia walked over. "I take it that you failed on your mission and have already accepted defeat."

Lazily, Nick opened one eye and used it to send a lingering gaze down her legs. She had to go find a longer skirt. Better yet, pants.

"Not at all," he murmured in a voice so perfect it sounded manufactured. "I've already accomplished my mission, and I was merely waiting for the full hour to give you a fighting chance."

"Sure you were."

"Have a seat, Miss Sarcasm." He waved a hand at the hammock beside him.

Olivia had never been able to swing idly in a hammock. For one thing, she didn't do idle. She was a multitasker of the highest order. She listened to audio books while on the treadmill, ate her meals at her desk, made verbal notes on her recorder while driving back and forth from interviews. She'd even written her articles on her laptop while sitting beside her mother during her chemo treatments.

For another thing, she'd never learned the art of how to slide gracefully into and out of a hammock.

"I'll just stand. What did you find out about Honey?"

"I'm not talking until you take a load off."

"There's no need for me to 'take a load off' as you so eloquently put it."

He said nothing, just closed that one eye and rocked back and forth, the ropes of the hammock creaking softly against the bark of the palm trees.

She gave an exaggerated sigh. "Fine," she muttered, "I'll sit in the damned hammock."

"You need to learn to relax, Honey."

"Stop calling me that."

"What do you want me to call you? Sweet Cheeks? Can't very well call you Olivia."

"Don't give me any dopey monikers. Don't call me anything."

"Whatever you want."

"Don't patronize me, either."

"I'm never going to win with you, am I?"

"Not likely."

"You know, I would have expected an objective journalist

to be…oh, I don't know, more objective. You've already got me tucked into a nice little box in your head and you're not letting me out of it."

"I've read your blog, I've talked to people and I've formed an intelligent opinion about your exploits."

"My blog persona is not who I really am. I'm surprised that you don't get that."

"Gee, so you're not a gadabout playboy? My bad. You really are out there saving the world, feeding starving orphans and such."

"There's nothing wrong with pure entertainment. It helps people get through the day."

"Numbs their brains in other words." Even as she said it, Olivia didn't really believe it. Entertainment did help people decompress. What was it about him that rubbed her the wrong way? How could he make her feel like a dullard with just a few laconic words and one of his knowing glances?

"You're right," she admitted, which was as much of an apology as she was prepared to give. "I'm not objective when it comes to you."

Both eyes popped open and a sly smile edged up the corners of his mouth. "Excuse me, I thought I heard an apology in there somewhere."

"Don't make me regret saying it."

"Okay," he said and shut up.

"So about Honey…"

"You want what I've got, then park your fanny in the hammy."

"That's too cute." She eyed the hammock, tried to figure out how she was going to get into it without her short skirt flipping up. "It's nauseating."

"I get it now."

"Get what?" She eased down, testing her weight on the flimsy sling.

"You."

"What about me?"

"You enjoy being contentious."

"I do not." Did she?

"You're contentious right now."

"I—" She snapped her mouth closed. She *was* being contentious.

"What makes you so scrappy?" he asked.

"I like to win," she confessed.

"Let me guess. Debate team in high school."

"And college."

"You gonna perch on the edge of that hammock all afternoon or are you going to stretch out?"

"Do I have to?"

"Yes."

Okay, she supposed it wouldn't kill her. What's the worst that could happen? That she would flip over, fall on the ground and Nick would get a terrific view of her pink boy-short panties. Undignified yes, but it could be worse. She could be wearing a thong.

With her fingers laced through the webbing of the hammock, she shifted, swinging her legs around, trying to keep her knees pressed together. The hammock wobbled precariously. She was off balance and didn't know how to right herself.

She shifted, trying to correct the tilt, but only managed to make things worse. The hammock buckled. She was going down. She could feel herself losing control and the loss of control always panicked her. Scrambling, she tried to snatch at anything she could to stay level, but she could not find salvation. She braced for a fall.

Suddenly the hammock steadied.

"Easy does it."

She glanced over to see Nick had placed a hand on the hammock, holding it secure. His knuckles were lightly resting against her hip bone. Only the thin material of her clothes separated his bare skin from hers.

"Much as I'd love a glimpse under that skirt, I don't want to see you hurt yourself," he murmured.

"Short drop like that onto sand? Not much pain involved."

"I could take my hand away. Let you and the hammock fight it out." He smirked. His dark hair had flopped over his forehead and made him look all Jane Austen hero-y.

"No, no."

His rich, deep laugh curled around her. "You're a lot of fun, you know that?"

Olivia wrinkled her nose. She'd been called a lot of things, but fun wasn't one of them. Why did his comment feel so refreshing?

She peeked over at him. His gaze rested on her face, warm and inquisitive. He really was a good-looking guy. "So," she said, getting back to business. "I think an agreement is in order."

"An agreement," he echoed.

"That we don't scoop each other. I guess that your slant is on J.D. since you write about single men in Texas, and my slant is on Holly. We can both get our stories without upstaging the other as long as we release them at the same time."

"What's in it for me?" he drawled.

"Do you always have to be so difficult?"

"Only with you."

Olivia gritted her teeth. "Fine, what do you want?"

He didn't say anything for such a long time that Olivia thought he might have fallen asleep. "Go out with me when we get back home."

"No."

He shrugged. "All I have to do to publish my story is write it up, get my secretary to proofread it and hit Send. You, however, have to go through an editor. Scooping you is a no-brainer."

"I'll let you have the bed."

"I've already won the bed."

"What did you find out about Honey?"

"She's Holly's first cousin, but I suppose you discovered that on the internet." His hand was still beside her hip, distracting, and yet it was the only thing keeping her balanced.

"Uh-huh," Olivia lied.

"They were really close when they were little kids, but then Honey's parents—that is her real name by the way, apparently her mother was a beekeeper's daughter—became missionaries and took an assignment on an impoverished island in the South Pacific. It's an isolated place without the internet or even television. Honey went to college in Australia, but went back to the island to teach school. Honey and Holly haven't seen each other in twenty years, although they've occasionally written letters back and forth. Which explains why Holly mistook you for Honey since they haven't seen each other since they were seven."

"Surely they must have exchanged pictures over the years."

"They did, but apparently you're a dead ringer for Honey."

Olivia was impressed with Nick's research, but she didn't want him to know that. "How did you find all this out?"

"J. D. Maynard was just in that hammock."

"You didn't give yourself away, did you?"

Nick made a derisive noise. "Oh, ye of little faith. I know what I'm doing. I told him that you swept me off my feet when we met in Hawaii while we both were attending a teachers' conference and we'd gotten engaged after only knowing each other a couple of weeks."

"I've got to hand it to you—you're good."

"What's that? A compliment?" Nick cupped his free hand around his ear as if he couldn't believe what he was hearing. "Does this mean I get the bed?"

"You get the bed," she grudgingly conceded.

"Told ya. People research always trumps internet research," he boasted.

"For you, maybe. Bloggers have the luxury of using gossip. Print journalists can't be so cavalier. We have to triple-check our facts."

"You're insinuating that I never check my facts. That's elitist bullshit," Nick said. "Internet journalists aren't any less valid than print journalists. In fact, we're the wave of the future. You can't fight the tsunami. One day, you're going to be an internet journalist yourself or be dead in the water."

"You're not a journalist," she said. "You're a blogger. Big difference. Mostly you've been lucky all your life. Things just seem to fall into your lap."

The minute the words were out of her mouth, she regretted them. Nick's face fell and she could tell she'd hit a nerve. She knew he didn't have a degree in journalism, that he'd dropped out of college. What she hadn't known was how much that bothered him, but the expression in his eyes told the story.

"So about this no scooping each other thing," she said, back-tracking. "Here's what's in it for you. Holding back will prove your journalistic integrity. It will show me that bloggers are as good as print journalists."

"I don't have to prove a damn thing to you." He let go of her hammock and got out of his, coming to his feet to tower over her. He looked down and she felt her heart leap into her throat.

"Listen," she said, "I'm really sorry, I didn't mean—"

"Don't worry," he cut her off. "The bed is yours. I wouldn't share a room with you if you paid me."

Olivia bailed out of her hammock, surprised at how easily she got up without tripping herself. She moved to block his way, hemming him in with the hammocks on either side of him, a palm tree at his back, and sank her hands on her hips. "Oh, no, buster. You won the bet, you take the bed."

"Get out of my way, *Honey*."

"I don't know why you're getting so testy, I'm the one who got hijacked to this island."

"Don't start blaming me again. You're a big girl. Accept responsibility for your actions. Now please step aside before I do something I'll regret."

Olivia raised her chin, pushing him, daring him. "Go ahead, do it."

He stalked forward. Olivia stood her ground.

"For the record, I won't scoop you because I pity you. Being a print journalist in this day and age has reduced you to pathetic insults. Keep on clinging to that journalistic integrity crap. It's all you've got to keep you afloat."

"Oh, yeah?"

"Yeah."

He peered into her eyes. She absorbed the punishing stare. All moisture drained from her mouth. The next thing she knew, he had snugged her up tight in his arms, yanked her off her feet and kissed her with a power that sucked every ounce of air from her lungs.

Her head whirled. Her heart thundered. Her lips dissolved into the masculine maelstrom. He kissed her until she couldn't breathe and her world tilted upside down.

"There," he said, pulling his lips away and setting her on her feet. "Let that be a lesson to you."

YOU ACTED LIKE A BIG JERK. Nick scolded himself. *Olivia didn't say a word that wasn't true, then you kissed her for no damned good reason and stormed off like a sensitive tit.*

Which wasn't like him at all—insults usually rolled right off his back—but when Olivia spoke the truth, it hurt. Not because he hadn't finished college. He could go back anytime he wanted. No, what stung was Olivia's disregard because he hadn't followed the traditional channels. He hated that she didn't take him seriously.

Come on, can you really blame her? You work hard at getting people not to take you seriously. Even the name of your blog, Man About Texas, is all tongue-in-cheek. She's taking you at face value. Why are you so upset?

Yeah? Why was he letting her get to him? Who the heck was Olivia Carmichael?

Just the heir apparent to one of the most respected families in journalism, that's all.

Annoying, that's what she was. Never mind that things had been going well between them until he'd gotten all defensive. She'd even apologized, and he sensed that was not something Olivia did lightly.

"Hey, Nick!" J. D. Maynard called to him from a group of guys playing beach volleyball. "We're about to leave for the bachelor party. Wanna ride with me on my last night of freedom?"

"Absolutely." Nick had to agree with Olivia. Things did seem to fall into his lap. Take this whole situation for instance. He'd lucked into an all-expenses-paid vacation that stood to net him a book contract.

Half an hour later, J.D., Nick, a half dozen of his buddies and a couple of muscle-bound bodyguards jammed into the limo that took them to an entertainment compound in the middle of Rapture Island. Nightclubs and bars and restaurants ringed a big open-air pavilion packed with wealthy vacationers in festive clothing.

The air smelled of coconut, fried fish and buttered rum. Lantern lights strung from wires, winked on in the gathering dusk. Along a man-made lake, tiki torches were being lit. A cacophony of various musical venues clashed in a berserk duel of sound— reggae, calypso, zydeco, Latin rhythm.

J.D. led the way through the throng, headed for a gentleman's club situated in the back corner of the compound.

Ah, the ubiquitous strip joint. Just once, Nick would like to attend a bachelor party that wasn't in a strip club. He'd been going to a lot of them lately as one by one his friends had gotten hitched.

He realized he was the lone holdout among his group of friends. He was thirty now and everyone he hung with was engaged or married. When and how had that happened?

"So." Nick asked J.D. the question he'd been dying to ask him as they clambered up onto the boardwalk leading to the strip club. "How did you know, out of all the women in the world, that Holly was the one?"

J.D., who'd clearly already had a couple of beers during the volleyball game, wrapped an arm around Nick's shoulder and pulled him close as if they were best buddies from kindergarten. "Honestly, man, I love her like I've never loved another."

"Really? Never? But you've been with so many women and you could have any of them you wanted. Why Holly? How do you know she's really The One?"

And then J.D. shrugged, grinned and said the words Nick loathed hearing. "C'mon, you're in love. You just *know*."

5

HOLLY TOOK OLIVIA AND HER five other bridesmaids to a private luau where they were escorted through a big open-air pavilion surrounded by clubs and restaurants to a secluded beach area ringed with flaming tiki torches. Swarthy young men handed them mai tais, placed flower leis around their necks and kissed their cheeks. Olivia took a sip from her drink and puckered her mouth at the sweet potency. The bartender had been very liberal with the rum. The scent of roasted meats mingled with the fresh aroma of pineapple and plumeria blossoms. A trio of bongo players sat beneath palm trees pounding out a seductive rhythm.

Another swallow of her drink and Olivia was feeling the island beat. She swished her hips in time to the music. She'd made up her mind she was going to enjoy herself and forget all about Nick Greer and his stupid kiss that had rocked her universe.

But no matter how hard she tried to involve herself in the ongoing conversation about the wedding, her thoughts kept drifting back to that kiss. As far as kisses went, well, she just might have to add it to her list of favorite things. It had been like the ultimate chocolate chip cookie—rich, sweet, decadent and totally bad for you.

Knock it off. Yes, he's hot. Big deal. Unless you're in the market for a carefree fling.

Was she in the market for a carefree fling? She'd never had one before, but if she'd been contemplating it, Nick was the way to go. Fun, easy, breezy, absolutely no strings attached. Hmm.

She had to stop thinking like this. She knew better. Knew precisely what she was letting herself in for with a man like Nick, and yet, she could not stop tasting him on her tongue, could not stop feeling the brush of his beard stubble on her chin, could not get the intoxicating smell of him out of her nose. He was all around her.

Argh!

"Honey?"

Olivia blinked and yanked her hand away from her lips, which she hadn't even realized she'd been caressing. "Uh-huh?"

"You were daydreaming about Nick, weren't you?" Holly teased.

"Yes," Olivia admitted guiltily.

Holly reached across the table strewn with empty plates and glasses and touched Olivia's hand and gave her a secretive smile. "I know exactly what you're feeling. You'd rather be with Nick. I'd rather be with J.D. Remind me again why we're here and they're at the gentleman's club across the pavilion?"

Nick was across the pavilion? Olivia's heart gave a strange thump.

"One last night of freedom, woohoo!" one of the other brides-maids hollered and raised a triumphant fist. "And to watch the male strippers."

Holly rolled her eyes. "Please don't tell me you hired strippers."

"We did." Her girlfriends giggled.

At that moment, the bongo music stopped and the sound of "You Sexy Thing" came over the speakers mounted on the palm trees above their heads. For the next several minutes they were regaled with Chippendales-quality dancers as "You Sexy Thing" morphed into "You Can Leave Your Hat On." But after you'd seen one buff, near-naked man, you'd seen them all.

You haven't seen Nick naked.

A vision of Nick bumping and grinding and stripping off *his* clothes in time to the seductive music popped into her head, erotic and X-rated.

That's when Olivia realized she'd had one mai tai too many.

THE MEN LEFT THE STRIP CLUB long before midnight because J.D. was missing Holly. Nick made whip-cracking noises even as relief spread through him. He was ready to get back to the resort, find Olivia and kiss her again just to see if it would be as potent the second time around.

What the hell was that all about?

Their rowdy group started across the pavilion, but a crowd that had gathered around a street performance distracted them.

"Let's see what's going on," one of the guys said. "It's too early to call it a night just yet. This is your last chance to go balls-to-the-wall crazy, J.D."

"My balls are retiring from the wall." J.D. grinned, not the least bit ashamed when the whole group made whip-cracking noises. "They now belong exclusively to Holly. You'll all see one day. There's more to life than wine, women and song."

Nick joined the group in razzing J.D., but part of him understood what he was saying. Lately the single life was beginning to feel too routine, and sometimes late in the dark of night, he'd found himself wondering if there was something more. Of course, when the sun came up, he pushed the thoughts away. He made his living writing about being young, single and footloose in Texas.

Yeah, but how long are you going to be young? You can't be Peter Pan forever.

Peter Pan? He wasn't Peter Pan. He just liked having a good time. Nothing wrong with that.

Maybe not, but wouldn't you like something more substantial?

And just as the thought popped into his head, the crowd parted to let them pass and there she was.

Olivia.

Responsible, uptight, contentious Olivia…doing the limbo?

"How low can you go?" called out the DJ as the friendly limbo beat drummed into the thick, warm night graced with a full yellow moon.

Who would have thought it possible? The sight of Olivia, wild-haired and giggling as she shimmied underneath the limbo pole held aloft by two muscular island natives while "The Limbo" spilled from the outdoor sound system, gripped Nick. She moved as limber as an eel. How did such a rigid woman get so flexible? He liked this look on her—fun, uninhibited, slightly out of control.

One of the burly, pole-holding dudes was staring at Olivia as if she was an ice-cream cone he wanted to lick. Unexpectedly, a fissure of jealousy cracked open inside Nick. He had a startling urge to plant a fist in the guy's grinning mug. What was this? He'd never been the jealous type. He was the guy who felt a kick of pride whenever someone ogled the woman he was with.

Dude, you're not with her.

No, but he wanted to be and that foreign urge was far scarier than the jealousy.

Olivia stood up on the other side of the pole, cheeks flushed, hair tousled, eyes dancing. Her friends clapped enthusiastically, egging her on.

She was beautiful. Truly beautiful.

"Nick!" Her smiled widened when she spotted him and she waved.

Her friendly tone alarmed him. "You've been drinking."

She held up two fingers. "Just two. But they were—" She paused to hiccup, slapped a hand across her mouth, giggled, then hiccuped again. Olivia Carmichael could giggle? Who would have believed it? "Strong and I'm not accustomed to imbibing hard liquor and…" She swayed gracefully.

Instinctively he put out a hand to brace her.

She didn't move away from him. "Chivalry, Nick? That's unexpected."

"Tipsy, Carmichael? Equally unexpected."

She laughed, her bright eyes dancing.

"How low can you go?" dared the DJ.

"How low can *you* go?" Olivia purred.

Flustered and surprised by his lack of a quick comeback, Nick lowered his head, rubbed a palm across the back of his neck.

"Couples limbo," the DJ enticed.

Olivia held out her hand. "C'mon. Let's limbo."

"I can't believe you can do the limbo."

"Why not?"

"You don't seem the flexible type."

"Fifteen years of yoga, my friend. I'll kick your ass."

"Game on," he said, stripped off his jacket and handed it to one of J.D.'s buddies to hold. "Bring it."

The limbo song started over as couples lined up to slink underneath the pole two by two. The first couple didn't make it. A tall, ungainly guy knocked into the pole. The crowd laughed.

"How low can you go?" the DJ purred in a deep bass.

Another couple made it through, laughing as they went.

Next, it was their turn.

"Lower," Olivia instructed the pole holders.

The men flashed shining white teeth and lowered the pole an inch.

"Lower." Olivia motioned exactly where she wanted the height of the pole.

The men simultaneously raised their eyebrows. She was pointing at the level of their kneecaps.

"Yes," she confirmed.

Grinning and shrugging, they lowered the pole.

"Now," she told Nick, "let's win this damn thing."

Ah, there was the Olivia he knew and loved.

Loved?

Had he actually thought that ridiculous thought? Nick gulped.

Olivia grabbed his hand. "This is it, Romeo, show me what you've got."

In unison, they both leaned back and let their legs carry them low to the ground as they inched forward trying not to hit the limbo bar or lose their balance and fall backward.

It was too low.

Nick couldn't make it. He risked a glance over at Olivia and she was sliding underneath the pole like hot syrup. How the hell did she do that? The woman was as limber as a noodle. Who would ever have thought it?

He had to keep up. He wasn't going to let her get the best of him. He took a deep breath, marshaling the strength of his quadriceps to keep him aloft while at the same time easing his body forward. He wasn't going to make it. He was going to hit the pole and disappoint her.

"How low can you go?"

That DJ was seriously getting on his nerves.

"Nick be nimble," Olivia sang, changing the lyrics of the song to suit the situation. "Nick be quick."

Quick. That was it. He was moving too slowly. He needed to speed up, get under that pole as fast as possible.

Olivia was already through, on the other side waiting for him. The crowd started clapping in time to the rhythm.

With one last spurt of energy, he pushed his body clear of the pole. Then, exhausted, he collapsed onto his back, while simultaneously reaching for Olivia and pulling her down with him.

"Wow," she breathed as she gazed into his face. He wrapped his arms around her to the sound of the cheering crowd. "I had no idea you were that limber." She echoed his words back at him.

He looked her square in the eyes and in a deadpan delivery said, "Fifteen years of mattress yoga."

IT WAS NOT A CHARMING THING to say, but it didn't matter. Olivia was charmed.

All she could think about was how flexible he was and what dynamite physical chemistry they had going on between them. If she'd ever wanted a no-strings-attached sexual fling, now was the time and Nick was the perfect person to indulge with.

I want, I want, I want. Her body throbbed.

What the hell? Why not? They were sharing a bungalow. No one would ever have to know they slept together. One gloriously naughty weekend and then they could go back to their ordinary lives. Nothing would change.

"Nick, do you want to get out of here?" she shocked herself by asking.

"Honey," he said, "I thought you'd never ask."

THE GROUP ENDED UP MERGING their bachelor and bachelorette celebrations into one big bash. In the midst of it, Nick and Olivia wandered toward the beach. No one seemed to notice them slipping off. The sound of island music followed them as they walked and mingled with the whispering rush of the ocean. Wind stirred the palm fronds, ruffling Olivia's hair. The moon cast her profile in shadows, softening her features.

Nick reached out to take her hand, surprised by how much he wanted to touch her in this simple way.

She didn't withdraw as he feared she might. Instead, she allowed him to interlace their fingers. The charm bracelet around her wrist fell against the back of his hand. He fingered the charms one by one, five in all—a pencil, a computer, a quill, a parchment scroll and a miniature Pulitzer medal.

"I've never seen you without this bracelet on," he said.

"College graduation present from my grandfather. It's the last thing he gave me before he died."

"It puts a lot of pressure on you."

"What?" She seemed startled. "No. It's my touchstone. Keeps me on my path."

"Is it your path? Or is it the path your family set you on?"

"It's the same thing."

"Is it really?"

"Yes," she said staunchly, after a split-second hesitation.

He let the topic drop. The night had been magical and he didn't want to stir her up. He squeezed her hand as they walked and she squeezed back. Nick couldn't remember the last time he'd held hands with a woman. Had he ever held hands with a woman?

She was humming the limbo song under her breath.

"You're relaxed," he said. "It looks good on you. I get the feeling you never let your hair down."

"I don't much," she admitted.

"I like the mellow Olivia. You should let her out of the sweat-shop every once in a while."

"I'll take that under advisement."

He stopped walking. The pavilion was several yards behind them; the sound of merrymaking carried out into the night. She smelled like coconut and sea breeze and he wanted to taste her again more than anything else on earth. She pulled on his arm a bit, trying to tug him forward, but when he wouldn't budge, she came back.

"What?"

His gaze tracked over her face and he realized he was feeling something much deeper than lust. Something profound. Curiosity, mixed with heightened awareness, mixed with a craving that touched deep down into his very core. Looking into her sharp eyes sliced him to ribbons somewhere in the vicinity of his heart. What was it about her that had so taken his interest hostage? Was it her sense of drive and unabated passion for her work? Was it her wickedly subtle sense of humor? Or was it simply the fact that she could see through him like a pane of glass?

There could very well be something to that last part. He was accustomed to women falling all over him. But this one, this one...

She had his number and he found that strangely intoxicating. Whereas for her part, Olivia acted as though he was more an annoyance than anything else. Except for this moment. Right now, she seemed pensive instead of pent up. He had a strong urge to take advantage of her easier state of mind.

You are so screwed, Greer. She's too smart, too savvy, just too damn much woman for you.

"What?" she repeated impatiently. "What is it?"

"This," he said, pulled her into his arms and kissed her.

Her lips were even sweeter the second time. He'd known they would be. He shouldn't be kissing her. On the smartness scale, kissing Olivia Carmichael was right up there with juggling hot coals barehanded. But he thrilled to the lure of danger and right now, she was the most dangerous thing around.

That's all this is, he tried to convince himself, *the thrill of the chase.* Nothing more. He had nothing to be worried about. Right?

He tightened his grip on her and she twined her arms around his neck and the next thing he knew they were lying on the sand. Olivia's soft breasts were pressed against his hard chest. Nick's blood throbbed through his whole body. He wanted her so badly he couldn't think straight, and he was alarmed to discover his hands were shaking. He kissed her and kissed her and kissed her as if the world was going to end that night and this was their last chance to mate.

This is a really, really bad idea. Don't do it.

She'd been drinking and she was thinking with her body and not her head. If he made love to her tonight, he knew she was going to regret it in the morning and he didn't want to be responsible for making her feel lousy. Nick wanted her to feel every good thing in the world.

But while he was mentally putting on the brakes, Olivia kissed him hard.

It was all he could do to disentangle her arms from around his neck and pull his mouth from hers. The buttons of her blouse gaped open. Somewhere along the way he'd unbuttoned it and he didn't even remember doing it. "Listen, Olivia—"

"No talking," she murmured and captured his chin between her sassy teeth. "Just sex."

He ran a hand through his hair. This was insane. He couldn't be feeling the things he was feeling. It didn't make any sense. Not now. Not here. Not with Olivia Carmichael.

But one look in her eyes and he wanted to give her everything she asked for. "We can't do this."

Another time, another place and he'd have her naked within a New York minute, but not like this. He wanted his first time with Olivia to be special.

Special?

Where in the hell had that thought come from? What was happening to him? What was it about her that made him feel so…so…*noble?*

"Why not?" She reached for his belt.

"Olivia, no," he said gently and laid a hand on her wrist. Her charm bracelet jangled.

"Oh," she said. Her bottom lip quivered slightly, but she quickly clamped her bottom teeth on it. Her soft vulnerability bludgeoned him. "Oh, I'm such an idiot. You…you're not attracted to me. You don't find me sexy, or at least not sexy enough to sleep with me."

How could she possibly be thinking that? His cock was four hundred kinds of hard and it was all he could do to keep from stripping off her clothes and taking her right there on the beach.

"Woman," he growled and yanked her up tight against the length of him, making sure she felt his erection. "Does that feel like I don't think you're sexy enough?"

She tilted her head, her eyes widening. "Well…well…"

"Yeah, well. You've got me tied in knots and aching so badly that I can't breathe."

"So let's get naked."

"We can't."

"Why not?"

"You're tipsy."

"I'm not *that* tipsy." Her fingers played through his hair.

"Tipsy enough." He stepped away from her.

"C'mon, take advantage of the situation." She closed the distance between them. "Take advantage of me."

"I can't."

"Why not?"

"It's complicated. You're complicated."

"It doesn't have to be complicated. It could be sweet and easy. Like pie for dessert. Isn't that what you do? Isn't that you? Taker of the sweet and easy path."

God, how he wanted to ignore his noble impulses and just take her. "It's what I do. It's not what you do."

"Not usually," she admitted. "But this time, I want to. Just this once. Just one bite of sweet dessert. It doesn't have to mean anything. That's why you're perfect. I don't *want* it to mean anything."

Her words were a smart slap. His ears stung. She was interested in him simply because he had a reputation for casual relationships and she wanted a hot island fling. He stared at her, caught off guard by his hurt feelings. "Well, maybe I do."

6

—————

WELL, MAYBE I DO.

Nick's words still echoed in Olivia's head two hours later after they'd returned to the resort in the limo with the others. What did that mean? Could Nick honestly want something more from her than a short, hot affair? Really? Nick Greer? But how was that possible? She couldn't wrap her head around it. Couldn't trust it. In spite of her doubts, her heart strummed with excitement. Nick wanted her.

He's never been in a committed relationship. He doesn't know how to have one. Even if he's not deluding you, he's deluding himself.

Olivia lay on the bed at the resort, feeling hot and achy and disappointed and sad and hopeful and worried and a million other different things. Nick had insisted she take the bed, even though the cool night breeze was probably what she really needed to soothe her heated skin.

What was happening to her? It had all started when she hadn't opened her mouth to tell Holly Addison the truth about who she was. She'd compromised her moral integrity, and now she was no longer sure who she was or what she wanted, and it was all so confusing. Especially since she'd had more fun in the past twelve hours than she'd ever had in her life. Unbelievable as that sounded, it was true. Whenever she was around Nick, she felt lighter, happier.

For years she'd been pushing herself to excel. And then just when she'd been about to achieve her goals, her mother had gotten sick and she'd walked away from the *Washington Post* and come home to take care of her. She didn't resent or regret it, but of late, her mind had been on dark things and Nick offered her a breath of fresh air.

An escape.

Ultimately, was that what attracted her to him? Could it be that he was a release valve for her moody, broody thoughts? Or was it that he was just downright sexy as sin?

Yes. The answer was yes. That was why she'd wanted a fling with him. But Nick had suggested that he wanted much more than that with her.

Question was, what did she want?

She didn't want to get hurt and she didn't want to hurt Nick.

Funny, she'd never thought she would agree with Nick, but he was right. It was a good thing they hadn't had sex on the beach—a very good thing indeed.

So why then did she feel so cheated?

Get your mind off Greer. Tomorrow throw all your focus on Holly, get her story, get out of this romantic place and soon enough Nick will be nothing but a fond memory.

THE FOLLOWING MORNING, Olivia went with Holly and her bridesmaids to have their dresses fitted. It was easy enough milking Holly for information on how she and J.D. fell in love. Holly was nervous and when she got nervous, she chattered endlessly, plus she felt safe telling her "cousin" all the intimate details of their relationship.

The whole thing made Olivia uneasy, but she couldn't deny she'd managed to get an amazing story. She battled with her conscience, her journalistic mind warring with the part of her that truly liked and admired Holly. Whatever friendship they'd formed under these false circumstances was bound to be destroyed by the article, even if it was a favorable one. As she and Holly and the bridesmaids ate lunch at a quaint French bistro on the cobblestone streets of Rapture Island, she had a strong impulse not to use the story, to call Ross and tell him she'd come up empty-handed.

What would her grandfather do under the circumstances?

It was a rhetorical question because she knew what he would do. With Grandfather—and her father for that matter—the story always came first. Friendships and even family a distant second.

For the briefest of moments, she pondered the values that had been instilled in her since birth, that following the truth of a story was the noblest thing to which she could ever aspire.

But now she had to wonder if people's feelings might be just as important. It was a conflict she'd never dreamed she would have.

With these thoughts on her mind, she arrived back at the bungalow late in the afternoon to find Nick wasn't there. Relieved not to have the distraction, she sat down and started writing the first draft of her article. She'd just finished it with barely enough time to spare before she had to dress for the wedding rehearsal, when her cell phone rang.

The caller ID identified Ross.

"Hello?"

"Well?"

"Well, what?"

"I haven't heard from you in over twenty-four hours. The rumblings are getting louder around here. The new round of budget cuts are official. Heads are going to roll. Did you get a chance to talk with Holly while she was in Austin? I hope the answer is yes because otherwise…" He trailed off, leaving the rest to her imagination.

Olivia hesitated, fingered the Pulitzer medal on the charm bracelet at her wrist and told the truth. "I'm on Rapture Island and the place is crawling with paparazzi, but I managed to get invited onto the Maynard compound. I'm beating out the competition. *Well, except for Nick.*"

"What?" His excitement was electric. "How'd you do that? Never mind, I don't want to know. I simply bow to your genius. You are a wunderkind."

Uneasiness rippled over her. She'd lied and connived and Ross was proud of her? It didn't seem something to be worthy of praise.

"What have you got?"

"The story of how she and J.D. met. Her fears, her hopes, her dreams, details about the wedding—"

"Written up?"

"Just finished a rough draft."

"I want to see it."

Olivia thought about her deal with Nick, their promise not to scoop each other. "The wedding isn't until tomorrow. I'll have more for you after that," she stalled.

"I just want to see if you're on the right track. With the brass breathing down our necks we don't want to give them any excuses to can us."

"You can't run it yet."

"I won't," he assured her. "I'm so damned proud of you. I knew hiring you was one of the smartest things I've ever done."

"All right," she agreed reluctantly.

"Good girl," Ross said.

"I have to go now, I'm in the wedding party and we're about to leave for the rehearsal dinner."

"You're in the wedding party? Damn, but this is going to be good. Send me the article before you leave for rehearsal."

"I'm doing it now." With Ross's praise ringing in her ears, she logged onto the internet, attached the article to her email and pressed Send.

"SO REALLY," NICK SAID TO J.D. as they were getting their tuxes tailored for the wedding. "Why Holly, why now?"

J.D. looked at Nick as if he was a lost soul. "Are you having doubts about your relationship with Honey? Because if you are, don't go through with the wedding. If she's not the one—"

"It's not Honey," Nick surprised himself by saying. "She's a wonderful woman."

"But?" J.D. asked, giving a tug at his sleeves as he examined the tailored tux in the mirror.

"It's me."

"Ah," J.D. said. "You are madly in love with her."

Nick startled. He couldn't deny that he was in love with Olivia because J.D. thought she was Honey. He needed this interview. He needed job security. He needed that hefty contract his publisher promised if he could deliver on an interview with J. D. Maynard Jr. on the eve of his wedding. "Yeah," he said, surprised that instead of feeling like a lying fraud, a warm, gentle sensation wrapped around him.

"You're where I was about six months ago."

"So you did have doubts!"

"Not about my feelings for Holly," J.D. said, stepping down off the wooden stool and shrugging out of the jacket. He handed it to his tailor, while Nick's tailor was still busily pinning the hem of his high-dollar tuxedo pants. "But about my abilities to make her a good husband. She's a wonderful woman and she deserves the best."

"You were afraid you couldn't be loyal to her," Nick guessed.

"Not at all." J.D. smiled.

"But you went out every night. Had women hanging from both arms," Nick said.

"Gold diggers, celebrity chasers...no one real."

"And Holly's the real deal?"

"You better know it. Just like Honey is the real deal for you. Let me ask you something, Nick."

"Yeah?"

"What do you want most in life?"

This interview. Nick shrugged. "To be happy."

J.D. laughed. "But what does that look like?"

"A Ferrari in the garage?"

"That's not real happiness and you know it."

"Dude, you're dangerously close to sounding like a Hallmark commercial."

"It is the day before my wedding. I'm allowed."

"True."

J.D. cocked his head. "Do you want to hear my read on you?"

Might as well. Get some besotted love advice from J. D. Maynard Jr. "Sure."

"You're like me, an intensely loyal person."

He was? Nick squirmed.

"Don't move!" the tailor admonished fiercely.

Nick thought about his loyalties. He was loyal to his family. He went to dinner at his parents' house every Sunday evening without fail, unless he was out of town. He'd never missed his nieces' and nephews' birthdays. If any of his sisters ever called him, night or day, he was there. He loved them with an intensity that scared him. He thought of the friendships he'd had in his life. He tended to keep those light. In grade school, he'd had a best friend who was like a brother, and then Peter's family had moved away and Nick remembered feeling true grief at the loss.

And then there was Max. He remembered the old coonhound who'd dogged his every step from when he'd gotten him on Christmas the year he turned six until the day Max had died on Nick's high school graduation. Now that had been pain. It had hurt so much losing his best buddy in the whole world. Even now, just thinking about that dog made him tear up and he had the strongest urge to run out of the tuxedo shop and go do something to distract himself. Parasailing, hang gliding, making love to Olivia.

"Yes," J.D. went on, "you're so loyal that when you make a commitment to someone, it's for the duration. You'd lay down your life for the other person without blinking. But that kind of loyalty doesn't come cheap. When you commit yourself to something you stay committed."

Nick felt J.D.'s words all the way to his bones. It was as if the other man had looked at him and seen his every secret. It was startling and unsettling.

"What was your life like before you met her?" J.D. asked.

"Um…I have a wide circle of friends."

"You partied a lot. Just like me."

"And now?"

"Now I understand what I was doing."

"Which was?"

"Hiding from the pain that I knew commitment would bring."

"You're not afraid now?"

"Nope."

"Why not?"

"Because the thought of being without her hurts a hundred times more."

It was crazy, but Nick understood what J.D. was saying. He'd avoided falling in love because he knew that once he did, he would be the most dedicated person on earth. That level of commitment made you vulnerable. Every time the one you loved got hurt, it was worse than a hit to your own body.

"Time to man up," J.D. said. "Time to feel the pain and know that it's a good thing. Without accepting that pain is a part of being deeply in love, you'll never grow up."

"That's twisted, man."

"And the truest thing I've ever told anyone."

THE WEDDING REHEARSAL was fun and romantic. The dinner afterward was lavish. Nick got to meet J. D. Maynard Sr., one of the richest men in Texas and the rest of J.D.'s large family. He learned that, other than her cousin Honey, Holly had no immediate family. Her parents had both passed away and she'd been an only child.

But all through the rehearsal and dinner, Nick hadn't been able to keep his eyes off Olivia and he kept thinking about what J.D. had said to him. When they got back to the bungalow, he immediately went to the hammock on the beach because he knew that if he stayed in the room with her, he'd make love to her.

Around midnight, the moon vanished behind a heavy cloud that had rolled in. The air lay thick, sultry. Nick lay in the hammock rocking back and forth, trying to will away his boner.

It was a losing battle.

Every time he closed his eyes, he saw her. Her full pink lips, those sweet round cheeks and that tumble of blond hair twining down her shoulders. He recalled their kiss from the night before and he tasted her on his tongue—the nectar that was Olivia—a little tart on top, but soft and sweet underneath. He smelled her scent—like sunshine and flowers and cotton. He heard the sound of her voice, challenging him in the way no one had ever challenged him. She mixed him up and turned him around. Why did he love feeling so lost?

The wind kicked up, swaying the hammock with a sultry breeze. Maybe sleeping with her would cure the need. Maybe she was right and it was just all hot chemistry. *We aren't cut out for a relationship. She's a cat, you're a dog. Natural enemies. Besides, you're not long-term relationship material.*

Why not?

Why couldn't he have a long-term relationship? Where was it written in stone that he had to stay single just because he made a living blogging about the single life? He could change the direction of his blog to reflect the changes in his life. Change was a good thing, right?

Nick sucked in a deep breath. Did he want to change? Was he

really ready to pursue something more meaningful? Was Olivia really the one?

Overhead, the clouds rumbled and fat drops of rain fell from the sky.

OLIVIA WAS WIDE-AWAKE when she heard the back door slide open and the sound of rain rustling the vegetation, but she pretended to be asleep. Her heart started pounding like a bank robber on the run, beating so hard that she feared Nick could hear it in the silence of the room. She had her eyes closed, barely able to resist the urge to peek at him from behind her eyelashes.

He sank down on the other side of the bed.

Every muscle in Olivia's body tensed as she waited and waited and waited until finally she couldn't stand it one minute more. "Are you ever going to say anything?" she asked.

"I think we should just face this thing head-on," he said.

She sat up. "What thing?"

"Don't even try to pretend what's going on between us doesn't have you as jumbled up as it has me."

"I don't want to be jumbled up."

"Neither do I, but damn it, I am." Nick blew out a breath. In the darkness she heard rather than saw him shove a hand through his hair. "So let's not do it. You were right last night. Bad idea."

"Granted, it might be unwise, but I want you so badly I can't think straight and I'm pretty sure you're just as addled as I am."

"More so." Olivia's toes curled in anticipation. This felt crazy, illogical, out of control, and she loved it.

"What can I say, Olivia, is this feeling is all new to me."

"Why me?"

"I wish to hell I knew. You're confusing and confounding and irritating but whenever I think about you, I smile."

"Yeah, well thinking about you makes me smile, too."

"I don't want to hurt you."

"I don't want to get hurt."

"So where do we go from here?"

They sat in the darkness for a long silent moment, the wind buffeting rain against the terrace door. Olivia's head swirling, her body throbbing, her sex crying out for him.

"Olivia?" he whispered.

"Nick."

He reached out across the mattress and then she was in his arms. He tugged her into his lap, his lips weighed heavily against hers, his tongue languid and warm. Her pulse slipped through her veins brilliant as mercury—cool and quick.

Her body heated up, her nipples beading even harder as his erection pressed against her bottom. The man was big. Bigger than anyone she'd ever been with and she was both thrilled and nervous.

"You are such an intriguing woman," he murmured. "You had my attention for months, but I always felt you were too uppity to give me the time of day."

"I was," she confessed.

"Why the change of heart?"

She shrugged. "Getting to know you better. That playboy shtick is just a front. You hide behind it because you're afraid of anything deep and meaningful."

"I could just be a jerk."

"You're not."

He reached out to brush her hair from her forehead. "You have no idea how much it means to me to hear you say that."

Their mouths melded in a fresh surge of passion. Olivia had never in her life wanted a man as much as she wanted Nick. Any lingering misgivings disappeared in the thrust of pure sensation. Nick's tongue explored her and she volleyed back, an equal partner in the erotic duel, kissing him with a force so all-consuming she felt as if she'd been swallowed by the universe.

Silently, they undressed each other. He slipped her sleep shirt over her head. She yanked at the waistband of his cotton shorts.

His palms skimmed over her body, caressing her breasts, her waist, her hips. She licked his skin, salty with sea air and delighted in the taste of him. Ravenously he kissed her and Olivia unfurled, coming fully alive, throbbing with the tympanic tempo of escalating hormones. Her fingers trembled with anticipation, her muscles tensed, anxious for more of him.

Nick speared his fingers through her hair, held her still while he branded more kisses over her face. Touching his lips to her forehead and eyelids, cheekbones and chin—nibbling, sucking and licking.

Then when he lowered his mouth to capture first one nipple and then the other, Olivia let out a low, soft moan of intense pleasure. Her muscles tightened and her body caught fire.

"Do you have protection?" she whispered.

"On that score, call me reliable," he said, leaning over to search through the pocket of his shorts, which lay discarded on the floor.

After a quick fumble, he got the condom in place and then Nick lay back and pulled her on top of him. Olivia straddled his waist; her knees dug into the covers, his throbbing erection pressing hard against her bottom.

An excess of sensations washed over her—the husky sound of his breathing, the heat of their bodies pressed together, the scrape of his whiskers as he claimed her mouth in another demanding kiss.

A whirlpool of sinful pleasure carried her away on a turbulent tide of passion whipping high, increasing the sexual intensity that had been building since the moment she'd faced off with him at the Austin airport.

He tasted hearty, manly. Their tongues teased, sliding in and around and over each other.

She had a fierce urge to stroke him, to travel the tempting terrain of his body. Her hand, suddenly mischievous, slipped lower. She ran her fingertips over his belly, exalting in the way his taut stomach muscles quivered at her touch. His low groan fired her engines.

She traced a trail to the long, hard length of him.

Exhilaration stirred her blood. "Mmm," she murmured at the feel of his hardness in her hand. "Mmm, you feel so good."

"I gotta have you, Livvy," he crooned, giving her a nickname that snatched at her heart. Only her family called her Livvy.

Joyfully Olivia descended on him, gasping as he filled her up completely. A groan tore from his lips. Pleased that she'd so unhinged him, she ground her pelvis against him.

Nick reached his other hand up to thread his fingers through her hair and guided her face down to his so he could capture her lips in a fierce kiss. Then he carefully flipped them over so they stayed fused. He was on top now and she happily relinquished control. His mouth captured hers as he thrust into her. Pushing hard and faster.

Nick couldn't breathe. There were no words to describe the incredible feeling of being inside her hot, moist body. His cock pulsed.

Olivia moved over him, eyes on his, her long blond hair falling over her face. He wrapped his hands around her waist, guiding her rhythm, watching with fascination as her gorgeous breasts jiggled. Each stroke brought him closer…and closer…and closer to bliss.

He fought the urge to come. It was a fierce battle—the way she was contracting her tight little box around him was almost more than he could bear. He had to clench his jaw and close his eyes and concentrate on making sure her pleasure was as great as his. He lightly pinched her nipples between his thumb and forefinger and she went wild, thrashing and writhing. "Nick, Nick, Nick."

"Livvy," he breathed and in spite of all the living he'd done, he felt as if he'd just been born. He was clean and fresh and new.

"Nick…I'm about to…I…I…"

"That's it, come for me. Let yourself go."

"I want to wait. I want you to come with me."

"For once you don't want to best me?" He chuckled.

"Well, put like that…"

"Beat me to it, Livvy."

She thrust her hips upward, pushing him to the limit. He clenched his jaw to hold back his own orgasm, determined she would enjoy her climax to the fullest before he let loose, but hearing her cry out in ecstasy triggered something primitive inside him. Instinct tensed his muscles for a hard primal thrust and as she screamed his name, he pumped into her with an urgency he'd never experienced.

And when it was over he held her in his arms until they both fell into an exhausted sleep.

7

THE MORNING SUN WARMED Olivia's face and she started grinning before she ever opened her eyes. Last night she'd made love with Nick three times and it had been the hottest sex of her life. Her grin widened. He had a reputation as a great lover and he'd certainly lived up to it. She stretched, yawned and glanced over to his side of the bed.

It was empty.

He took off on you.

A moment of panic slipped a knife into her heart. Then she immediately corrected the doom-and-gloom voice nibbling at the back of her mind. So what? This was a no-strings-attached fling. She didn't expect him to wake her up with a kiss and a snuggle. That would have been too romantic. She didn't need romance from him. Simple hot sex was fine by her.

Just when she was just about to buy into her propaganda, Nick appeared at the sliding glass door, a tray in his arms. His face lit up when he saw her. He winked.

She got up, wrapping the sheet around her—yes, he'd seen every inch of her last night, but now she was feeling a little shy—and padded to the door.

"Breakfast in bed," he announced.

A flush of alarm flashed through her. He was romancing her!

And she liked it. A lot.

No, no, no.

But the encouraging smile on his face and the delicious aroma of maple syrup, Belgian waffles and bacon had her scurrying for the bed. How did he know that Belgian waffles were her favorite?

It's probably just his go-to menu for the morning after.

Once she was back in the bed, covers tucked around her naked body, Nick stretched out on the mattress beside her. Giddy goose bumps raised on her arms. He pulled a small square box from his pocket and laid it on the tray beside the single red rose in a bud vase.

"What's this?" she asked, her throat constricting.

"Just a little something I picked up in the gift shop while I waited on the breakfast." He shrugged. "Go on, open it."

"I can see why you have such a reputation as a Romeo. Breakfast in bed on the morning after, gifts. Seduction 101."

"You've got such an erroneous impression of me."

"Hmm. I wonder how I came by that impression? Oh, could it be because you blog about your conquests?"

"I don't blog about my conquests."

"You so do!"

"I blog about what it's like to be a single guy in Texas."

"Which includes conquests."

"I never name names."

"How noble of you."

"Are you going to open the present before you make me regret getting it for you?"

"If it's expensive jewelry, I'm not keeping it. I'm not that kind of woman."

"You seem to think I'm a throwback to some 1960s Dean Martin romp. Want me to wear an ascot and mix martinis?"

She eyed him and the mystified look on his face had her laughing. He was right. In her mind, she'd created a slick, playboy image of him that didn't really fit with the fun-loving, easygoing man beside her. She picked up the box, untied the crisp pink ribbon and removed the lid.

Nestled on a bed of soft cotton lay a silver charm of a hammock strung between two palm trees.

"As a reminder," he said. "To slow down and enjoy life a little. All those charms on your bracelet are about work. You need something to balance you out."

"Oh," she said, feeling breathless, and she had no idea why.

"Here." He reached over to pluck the charm from the box. "Give me your wrist and I'll put it on for you."

She stuck her hand out and his fingers went to her charm bracelet. He opened the clasp on the palm tree charm and attached it to the bracelet between the Pulitzer medal and the miniature computer. His fingers were warm against her wrist and over the aroma of her breakfast she could smell his enticing masculine scent. Her stomach somersaulted.

"There," he said, let go of her wrist and leaned back.

He looked so comfortable against the pillow, his dark hair a sharp contrast to the white sheets. His gaze hung over hers, that sweet expression on his face making her feel downright loopy with joy.

"Livvy?"

"Yes?"

"You look so damn sexy right now." His words sounded heartfelt. "All rumpled and naked and amazing. You're better than I ever dreamed."

"You dreamed about me?"

"Almost constantly since you read me the riot act in McGulicutty's. Do you know how few women tell me off?"

What did he mean by that? Had he really being dreaming of her? If she were being honest, she'd admit she'd had a dream or two about him herself.

Uncertain of how to process her feelings, Olivia dug into her waffles. Nick reached over to filch a slice of bacon from her plate. The moment felt so cozy—too cozy for people who were having nothing more than a weekend fling.

She didn't know what to do or what to say. Part of her kept hoping…hoping for what? A real relationship with Nick? That was absurd on so many levels. And yet he wasn't at all like she'd thought he was. On the outside he might be a smooth operator, but on the inside beat a heart of gold.

Can you really take a chance on that?

A knock sounded on the door and relief surged through her.

"Olivia Carmichael, you open this door right now," Holly Addison commanded, the anger in her voice cold as a steel blade.

Panic hit into her as her eyes met Nick. "We've been found out," she said, her worst fear coming true.

"Don't worry," he said. "It's my fault. I take full responsibility."

"I'm as culpable as you," she said, shoving the breakfast tray aside and scrambling for her clothes. "We take this licking together."

Holly kept pounding. "Open this door right now or I'll knock it down."

Nick went to answer it. Olivia pulled up her skirt, smoothed down her hair. Hand on the knob, he hesitated, looked at her, waiting for her go-ahead. She nodded. He opened the door.

Holly came tumbling inside, eyes blazing, a fax of a newspaper article held in her fisted hand. "Explain yourself!"

"I…I…" Olivia stuttered. "What is it?"

With trembling hands, Holly smoothed out the paper and read aloud from it, "'J. D. Maynard and Holly Addison, match made in heaven or just the ultimate publicity stunt? By Olivia Carmichael.'" Holly wadded up the paper again and shook it under Olivia's nose. "How dare you pretend to be my cousin Honey. How dare you write such things about me?"

"I…I…" Olivia blinked. The headline came from the side notes she'd written to herself before she'd ever met Holly and J.D. A sick feeling settled in her stomach. Ross had lied to her. He'd taken her notes, turned them into an article and published it after he'd promised he wouldn't.

Except the nausea roiling inside her couldn't be as bad as what Holly must be feeling. "I'm sorry," Olivia apologized, "I'm so, so sorry."

"There is no excuse for what you've done," Holly said. "I've called security. They'll be here any minute to escort you from the premises."

But Holly wasn't the only one feeling betrayed by Olivia. "Let me see that," Nick said and snatched the printout from Holly's hand. He read it, raised his eyes and looked at Olivia with the most hurt expression she'd ever seen on a man's face. "This is this morning's edition of the *Austin Daily News*. You made me promise not to scoop you and then you went behind my back and scooped me?"

"Nick." She extended her hand.

"Here, I'm supposed to be the untrustworthy one and you blindsided me. What an idiot I am."

"Please, let me explain."

"There's nothing to explain," he said, backing away from her. "I get the message loud and clear. You'll do anything for your career. Even sleep with me to lull me into a false sense of security."

"That's not how it was," she said miserably, knowing he was not going to believe her.

"You're a reporter, too?" Holly blinked.

"No," Nick said. "Just ask Olivia. I'm nothing more than a college dropout who lucked into a successful internet blog." And with that, he turned on his heels and walked out.

OLIVIA SAT IN THE AIRPORT waiting for the next commercial flight back to the States, blinking away tears. What a difference two days made. She thought of all that had happened. All that she'd lost. She'd called Ross to confront him. The man was old-school journalism and he didn't apologize for what he'd done. All he'd said was, "It was a killer story. I ran it early to save our jobs."

"You hurt a lot of people," she said.

"Did I?" he accused. "You wrote it."

She realized he was right. It was her fault. Every bit of it. From pretending to be Holly's cousin, to scooping Nick. She should have taken a stand. She had not.

To comfort herself, she fumbled for the Pulitzer medal, but instead her fingers found the hammock charm. Balance. The charm Nick had given her was supposed to represent balance. Of which she had none in her life.

They'd been working on something and she'd gone and ruined it all by sending Ross that article. Hadn't part of her known he was capable of using it exactly the way he had? Had her subconscious sabotaged her?

It was a miserable thought. Was she that afraid of falling in love?

Love.

She took a deep breath. No matter how much she'd tried to tell herself it was just sex, she knew she was starting to fall in love with Nick Greer.

Well, that was all over now. Anxiously she rubbed the hammock charm as if it was Aladdin's lamp and she could conjure a genie to grant her most heartfelt wish.

To start again with Nick.

"Is that your touchstone?"

At the sound of his voice, she jerked her head up.

She turned to see him standing behind her in the terminal, his chocolate gold eyes studying her with intent. "Nick."

"Livvy."

"I sent my editor my notes," she said. "I made him swear not to publish it before I gave him the go-ahead but—"

"Shh," he said and crossed the space between them. "It doesn't matter."

"You forgive me?"

"Forgive you? I should be thanking you."

"Thanking me for scooping you when I made a promise I wouldn't?"

"It's all right."

"No. No, it's not. Now you'll have trouble getting your book contract and—"

He shook his head. "I got another idea for a book. I called my publishers and they've agreed to a contract."

"You came up with an idea that fast?"

"Getting punched in the ego can really kick the muse into gear."

"What's your new book about?"

"A perennial playboy and career-focused journalist go undercover at a celebrity wedding and fall madly in love."

"Love?" she whispered. "You love me?"

He wrapped his arm around her waist, pulled her against him. "I love every maddening thing about you, woman. How you finger that charm bracelet when you're feeling insecure. How you barrel fearlessly after your goals. How you're so loyal to your friends you're willing to make a spectacle of yourself in McGulicutty's bar. How you're a limbo star. That's seriously impressive."

"You only want me for my moves," she teased, her heart taking wing.

"No, I want you for your brains and your beauty, for your sharp tongue and your sweet lips. I want you in my life, Olivia Carmichael and I'm not taking no for an answer."

"I'm not putting up a protest."

"For once," he said, then kissed her with a passion that stole her breath. He kept kissing her until the plane arrived, until the other passengers around them had gotten on the plane, until the gate agent called for final boarding.

Then he took her by the hand, led her onto the plane and they flew off into their future together.

* * * * *

PRIVATE PARTY

Wendy Etherington

To my Y Girls team. Burning calories with you
is my favorite way to start the day.

1

SEATED IN THE LOBBY of the posh and exclusive Rapture Island Resort, Tara Lindsey flipped through *Food and Wine* magazine and pretended to be engrossed in the pages she'd read at least twelve times already.

Foolproof method for roasting chicken? Got that. Ad for a new convection oven? Saw it, too expensive. "Wine Pairings For Every Occasion" had lent some interesting tips. The article titled "You, Too, Can Perform Molecular Gastronomy!" made her roll her eyes. Ah, probably not. At least not without some serious training or a liquid nitrogen tank.

Interview with her mother? Saw that first thing, as her celebrity chef parent had been the one to send Tara the magazine in the first place.

Tara turned the page on her eerie, if older, twin. She saw the same features in the mirror every morning—curly dark brown hair, bright blue eyes, heart-shaped face, camera-ready smile.

Well, not so much with the smile. At least lately.

Which was why she was staking out the lobby of the exclusive Caribbean resort that was the setting of the wedding between Holly Addison, statuesque blond A-list Hollywood actress and J. D. Maynard Jr., son of J. D. Maynard Sr., Texas cattle ranch billionaire and oil magnate.

It was the event of the year. Invitations had been hand-delivered. The paparazzi were in a frenzy to get an inside peek. Security was insanely tight.

Tara had gotten a reservation at the resort—one of the few hotels on the island—by using her mother's name.

Nearly thirty and still hanging on to Mommy's coattails? Embarrassing beyond belief. Still, the employees of her catering company—especially the ones she was likely to lay off if business didn't drastically turn around—probably didn't care about her humiliation.

As long as they got paid each week, anyway.

An overly thin woman with long, sleek black hair sank onto the sofa a few feet away. She cast Tara a speculative look. "Are you here for the...*you know?*"

"Wedding?" Tara whispered back.

The woman's gaze darted from side to side before she inclined her head in a surreptitious nod.

"Yeah," Tara returned, keeping her tone low even though her excitement level rose. The wedding event details were a closely guarded secret. The CIA should take notes. But this was just the opportunity she'd been waiting for. "We're not supposed to talk about it, are we?"

"No, but I've been on a shoot for the last eighteen hours, and I need a damn drink. This cocktail party can't start soon enough." Her head turned in the direction of the hotel's tropical-themed bar. "I'm usually fashionably late, of course, but in ten minutes, I'm storming the gates."

The dark-haired woman looked vaguely like an actress Tara had seen on a TV drama, but since she did more sautéing than viewing, she couldn't be sure. No doubt there'd be an avalanche of beautiful and famous people present for the weekend events, but Tara had bigger fish to fry than autographs and pics to post on Facebook.

She was never going to be comfortable in the public eye like her celebrity chef mother. All those zooming cameras made her nervous. The lack of a private life and the pressure to constantly up the last project would put her in a constant state of insomnia.

She was good at what she did—she cooked. The solitude, the hard work, the opportunity to teach her employees new techniques, the pleasure in making people happy by feeding them well—it was her calling.

Yellow Rose Catering was her baby, her life.

And yet Maynard Sr. hadn't wanted her to cater his son's wedding. He'd chosen Tara's competition, Posh Events, which, in her opinion, was overpriced and overhyped.

But losing this latest contract had been a brutal blow, and Tara intended to find out why she was so lacking. To save her business and her reputation.

It was either that or go back to being Mama's prep chef.

"Hey, don't I know you?"

Tara flicked her attention to the woman beside her. The inquiry wasn't a surprise. "My mother is Daisy Lindsey."

The woman impulsively grabbed Tara's forearm. "Oh, my God! I *love* her show. I can't eat anything she cooks, of course, but I swear I get orgasmic just watching." The woman craned her neck to look around the lobby. "Is she here?"

"Uh, well…not yet." The lie might have stuck in Tara's throat, except she was desperate, so most of her ethics had been stamped out by the growing column of red numbers on her company balance sheet. "Probably tomorrow."

The woman's smile turned dazzling.

Definitely an actress. No normal person had teeth or cheekbones that perfect.

"Would you mind taking down my cell number and calling me when she gets here?" she asked.

"Sure." Especially since the news about the cocktail party—and the fact that it was taking place right there in the hotel bar—was crucial information to Tara.

As she entered Scarlet Sheldon's information into her own cell phone, she assuaged the pang of guilt she experienced by noting a reminder to send the actress a signed copy of her mother's latest book.

Her mother wasn't coming to the wedding. She was shooting a series of shows in a tornado-ravaged town in Kentucky for the weekend. The woman might have a rib-roast-size ego, but she was always there for her devoted fans.

In desperate need of a drink, the actress headed toward the bar. With a confident cock of her hip and a few words, the burly security guard let her pass into the exclusive depths of the party.

So easy.

And yet not.

There was apparently a strict list of invitees—complete with picture IDs to coincide with names. But to find out what foods her devious competition had created and was serving behind that proverbial velvet rope barely twenty feet away, Tara needed to be on that list.

And yet she wasn't.

The burly guard looked fairly bored. Maybe she could bribe him. Her petty cash was running low, so that idea had to be considered carefully. Maybe she could seduce him.

But, well…*yuck*.

Angling her head, she considered his barrel-shaped body. He certainly looked as if he'd eaten a cheese-laden tray of lasagna or two in his life. He might mistake her for her mother—an advantage for once. But then her mother wasn't on the guest list, either.

If only she could have swallowed her pride and asked her mother for an invitation. But then that would have meant admitting the reason for wanting to attend the wedding, leading to how bad her business was, ending with how she was on the verge of bankruptcy and failure.

Yuck again.

Just then, another man in a dark blue suit approached Mr.

Burly. His thick, wavy hair was so black it was almost blue. He had a hard-edged jawline and full lips. He was taller— way taller—and wider at the shoulders but all muscle. And all business.

With his hand resting on the butt of a pistol in a side holster, his gaze swept the lobby with seeming casualness, but Tara had no illusions that he hadn't taken in every single detail. Did he pause on her? Did she look out of place?

Was it obvious she was about to crash his client's wedding?

She couldn't discern his eye color from this distance, but she found herself leaning forward to try to get a better look. He definitely paused then.

Though she turned away quickly, a tingle of attraction danced down her spine.

Perfect. This is just freakin' perfect.

She reached into her bag for her lipstick and a mirror, which she used to primp, even as she took neck-craning glances around the lobby, hoping to appear that she was waiting for someone.

Oddly, she was certain this subterfuge wouldn't fool Mr. Hot and Dark.

She rolled her shoulders. It wasn't as if she was trying to take secret photos of the bride, the groom or even the guests. She wasn't going to make a scene or an illicit pass at the celebrities. She just wanted to taste the hors d'oeuvres and sample the supposedly custom-made cocktails.

And find out how that suck-up hack Carla Castalono stole her booking.

When she had the courage to glance toward the security guys, the Big Boss had disappeared. *Finally, hope.* Moving quickly through the lobby, she looked for a seriously inebriated male.

Strangely, this wasn't a challenge.

She sat next to him and watched his gaze rove her legs, exposed by the short, sarong-style skirt she wore. She had decent legs—not movie star quality but still a benefit from rushing around the kitchen all day.

When the guy's bleary gaze finally reached her face, she turned on the megawatt celebrity smile she'd inherited. "Hey, do you know who's getting married here this weekend?"

He thrust his arm around her waist as his whiskey-laden breath brushed her cheek. "How 'bout you and me, darlin'?"

Tara laid her palms against the guy's chest and pushed back. "Ah, no. I—"

"We're destined to be together tonight," he said before attempting to shove his tongue into her ear.

Lurching to her feet, Tara fought for her composure. It wasn't the first time she'd had to deflect some inebriated idiot's fumbling, but it had been a while.

Is your business worth this?

She thought of her pastry chef, who was a single mom. Her prep cook, whose father had just been diagnosed with Type 2 diabetes.

She could always go crawling back to Mama. Her team didn't have that option.

Leaning forward, she forced a smile. "I was thinking more about Holly Addison."

Like a lightbulb, her mark's eyes brightened. "She's hot."

"She is indeed. Plus, she's here."

The bleary eyes struggled to focus. His gaze moved past her. "Don't see her."

"Oh, but you will." Tara pointed toward the bar. "She's having a big party here to celebrate her upcoming wedding." She slipped him a twenty. "Buy her a drink." She winked. "You know, one more for the road."

The guy squinted briefly at the bill in his hand, then rolled his shoulders, returned her wink and stumbled off.

I am not a criminal. I am not evil.

Repeating this mantra, she headed toward the entrance to the bar but remained some distance behind her distraction. While he monopolized the guard's attention, she slipped around a tiki pole and over a rail, vaguely hearing her "partner" make a fuss about not being allowed to buy Holly a drink.

They were old friends, you know.

Tara did her best to disappear among the crowd and hoped his whiskey-altered state was too severe to pick her out of a lineup.

I am not going to be arrested.

She added this to her list of mantras and made a discreet beeline for the food tables.

With the Maynard coffers footing the bill for the destination wedding, she studied the elaborately decorative spread. A massive steer ice sculpture was the centerpiece. Tacky but at least she understood that. The garnishes of artfully carved fruits and veggies, plus a spread of green and red leaf lettuce looked lovely and fresh surrounding selections such as rolled-up ham alongside cubes of bright orange cheese, a beef roast being sliced by a bored-looking guy in a white chef's coat and mini egg rolls that glistened with the grease they had been fried in.

People whose faces and bodies made or broke their careers weren't going to eat that stuff.

And where were the vegetarian options? Something for the vegans? Hell, the only thing green was the globby-looking wasabi sauce and the beds of lettuce made to look like something but really only plumping up the skimpy offerings.

Keeping her head down, she reluctantly put a sampling of each item on her plate. Everything was as she'd suspected—processed, greasy and tasteless. The wasabi sauce had more mayonnaise than spice, and the egg rolls had certainly and most recently been stored in the freezer section of a supermarket warehouse. Fine maybe for a beer-and-ball-game gathering at a neighbor's house, but this was J. D. Maynard Jr.'s one-and-only—presumably anyway—stroll down the aisle.

Discreetly, Tara laid her nearly untouched plate on a corner table. Maybe with celebrities as guests, Maynard had figured nobody would eat, so there was no point in hiring a first-rate caterer. Yet Carla's prices were notoriously higher than Tara's. So why wouldn't he have saved himself a buck or two if he didn't care about quality? Which, ironically enough, he would have gotten if he'd hired Tara and her team.

Still, there had to be somebody at this shindig who ate. Holly's aunt Mildred or J.D.'s uncle Jake, somebody's goat-ranching grandfather or a big-time producer who didn't have to worry about fitting into a size-zero gown every awards season. Wealthy people could afford the best, and she knew Maynard Sr.'s business reputation was stellar. Why would he settle? It was weird.

The bar was doing a brisk business. A lot of guests were holding pink-tinted drinks—and, gee, how embarrassing for the guys. Maybe all the effort had been put into the booze.

Smiling vaguely at those she passed, one of which was the bride in a supertight blue satin dress, Tara inched her way to the bar. As she got closer, she overheard a guest comment about the delicious and refreshing drink "that clever caterer" had developed especially for the bride called The Addy.

The bartender—looking much more harried than the roast carver—shoved the drink toward her, then quickly turned to the next in line, so Tara slunk off to a corner to sample the brilliant concoction.

Well, hell, it was a Tom Collins, probably with a drop of red food dye to make it appear pink.

That drink had certainly been around before Maynard Sr. bred his first head of cattle and certainly way before Holly Addison's glam staff had discovered the wonders of performance-enhancing cosmetic procedures and the advantages of marrying a billionaire's son.

Custom cocktail, my ass.

Still, it was the best thing she'd tasted all night, so she sipped as she watched the guests mingle around her. She recognized many faces from stage and screen and found herself reluctant to return to her solitary room. It was sort of like being backstage at a concert or on a movie soundstage.

But this wasn't her party in any sense of the concept.

With a reluctant sigh, she started to set her half-consumed cocktail aside, then, impulsively, threw back the remainder of the contents. She'd heard chatter that the bachelor-bachelorette parties would take place later that night, and she could hardly insinuate herself into that crowd. She could do little but go for a solitary walk on the beach and wonder why she was such a failure.

So maybe she should go for a jog on the beach, release some endorphins and not obsess over her potential financial demise.

Before she could remember if she'd brought workout gear, a strong hand wrapped around her upper arm. And before she could do more than gasp, she was forced out the back door of the bar and onto the patio.

Mr. Hot and Dark loomed over her. "Nice job, bribing the drunk."

Her head spinning, Tara looked into his annoyed, smoky gray eyes. A lump formed in her throat even as a wave of heat spread through her body.

Oh, yeah, he was hot. And he certainly was dark. And really hot.

But maybe there was a small chance she was going to be arrested.

2

SHE WAS TOO SURPRISED to be a professional crasher.

Wade Cooper stared into the wide blue eyes of his captive and instinctively knew she was no threat.

He released her arm from his grasp. "Name?"

"Tara Lindsey."

"You're not on the guest list."

"No, but my mother is…well, could have been."

He stared harder. She had beautiful, trusting blue eyes.

But he didn't trust anyone or anything. He'd spent six years on the Presidential detail of the Secret Service and many more years of training and service at the Treasury Department before that elite assignment. He was hardwired to be controlled and meticulous. To withstand all physical trials. To fire upon the enemy. To protect the security of the nation.

Now bouncer at a celebrity wedding was all he had.

"Who's your mother?" he demanded of the woman before him.

"Daisy Lindsey."

He searched his memory and came up blank. Actress? Singer? He had no idea. "She a friend of the bride or groom?"

"She's—" Those stunning blue eyes searched his with clear bafflement. "She's on TV all the time. She's a chef." When he still didn't respond, her gaze turned speculative, interested. "She owns restaurants in New York, L.A. and Chicago. She's prepared meals for heads of state."

Now he was interested. "Presidents?"

"Two."

"The last two?"

"Of course. She's only fifty-four. Who are you anyway?"

So Ms. Lindsey's mother had made it through the stringent White House security screening—provided his crasher wasn't a liar as well as sneaky. But Wade hadn't met Daisy Lindsey. At least not if she'd passed on those eyes to her daughter.

He wouldn't have forgotten those eyes.

Shaking off the unprofessional thoughts, he crossed his arms and gave Tara Lindsey a fierce glare. "Wade Cooper, Security Chief, and currently your biggest problem."

She licked her lips.

Her lips could win as many prizes as her eyes. Bee-stung— but not in a weird, collagen-injected way—and painted a glossy pale pink.

"Look," she said, "I'm not a regular crasher."

Amused, he nodded. "No kidding?"

Heading inside the bar, two buxom blondes brushed past him, sending flirty glances his way.

He ignored them.

"Could we go somewhere more private and talk?" Tara asked.

"I'm a little busy just now, Ms. Lindsey. I've got some of the boys fitting uninvited guests for cement shoes, and I need to supervise. They tend to get a little carried away with the torturous confessions."

She paled, and he regretted his empty threat. She certainly was a jumpy little thing.

He'd known from the moment he'd seen her lurking around the lobby what she was attempting to do, but he'd been curious enough, bored enough, to see how she'd go about it.

And he'd enjoyed watching her weave through the crowd,

looking uninterested in everything but the buffet. Then, after tasting, looking disgusted.

He'd assumed she was simply hungry and not a fan after photos and autographs, but if she could afford to get to this exclusive island, she would hardly need to steal her meals.

When she glanced around at the glossy, laughing people around her and flushed, he found himself softening. "Stay here," he said, pointing at the wooden deck where they stood.

After her nod, he walked inside the bar, gave the area a sweeping study, then stepped out again. To Tara, he gestured to the steps leading to the beach. "After you."

They walked a few yards in the cool, soft sand until they stood next to the volleyball court set up behind the hotel. Palms swayed in the breeze, and the blue-green water had turned nearly black with only the moon as a spotlight.

"I'm sorry. I know you're busy," she said, tilting her head back and meeting his gaze. "How tall are you?"

"Six-four."

"You seem bigger."

"Only because you're small."

"I'm not small. Five-nine with the shoes." Along with a bright yellow top and skirt, she wore gold high-heeled sandals, which she reached down and removed. "Sorry, my feet are killing me. I need my Nike runners."

When she'd straightened once again, she licked her lips, and he bit back a groan. This job had been ridiculously easy so far. He supposed it was time for a challenge. It seemed remembering his duty was tossing the alluring Ms. Lindsey out on her backside would be the one.

"I guess it wasn't hard to see I didn't belong at the party," she continued. "I really stand out as the plain Jane in this crowd of stars."

Personally, he didn't think she needed all the glitz and sequins to be beautiful. She simply was. "My targeting you had nothing to do with the way you look."

She cocked her head. "So what'd I do wrong?"

He simply shook his head.

"Fine, fine. Trade secret, huh?" She lifted one side of her mouth in a tempting smile. "I have a killer recipe for coconut cupcakes I could share in exchange."

"Make the cupcakes, then we'll see."

The grin widened. "Deal."

The smile had Wade clinging to his professionalism by a thread—a state he'd never found himself in. He'd lived his job for a long time and had a hard time with relationships. Women wanted closeness and sharing. He didn't get close or share.

"Before you officially toss me out, you should know I have a good reason for being here."

Wade glanced back at the door leading to the party, then shifted his gaze to Tara's and lifted his eyebrows.

She sighed. "Okay, so technically I'm already out."

"And you can't tell me you're here because you're a big fan of Holly Addison's."

"Why not?"

"You barely glanced at her when she walked by you earlier."

"I suppose I didn't."

"And you're not one of J.D.'s—Sr. or Jr.—exes."

"You don't think so?"

"I've seen a lot of them." He let his gaze rove her from head to toe. She had plenty of curves, but they were subtle and—he'd bet his Justice Department Commendation for Valor—real. "You're not the type."

"Why am I not flattered?"

"But you should be."

"You're very…enigmatic."

He nearly smiled. "Am I?"

"Definitely. Do you want to hear my sob story for crashing or not?"

"Until the bachelor and bachelorette parties start, I'm all yours."

"When's that?"

He flicked a glance at his watch. "Twenty minutes."

"Fine. Never let it be said I delayed scheduled debauchery by starlets and cattle ranchers." As she crossed her arms over her chest, her expression turned fierce. "I'm trying to save my business."

"What business?"

"I'm a caterer."

"That explains the tasting and grimacing."

"I'm starting to get a little creeped out by the idea that you've been watching me so closely for the last hour."

He shrugged. "It's my job."

"So you should understand why I'm trying to save mine—and those of my employees. The catering company Maynard Sr. hired for the wedding, Posh Events, has been swiping contracts from me for months. Sometimes they undercut my prices to the point that they have to be operating at a loss. But most times their prices are higher, yet they still get the booking instead of me. It's driving me crazy." She paced in a tight circle. "It's driving me out of business. So maybe I went a little overboard by coming here, but I had to find out what was so great about Carla and her Posh Events firsthand."

She fisted her hands at her sides as she faced him. "My food is good, Mr. Cooper. Maybe I'm not famous like my mother, but I know how to cook."

He held up his hand. "What does fame have to do with catering?"

She rolled her eyes as if to say *you wouldn't believe me if I told you*. "Reputation is everything in the food business. Serve a good meal, make one person happy. Serve a bad meal, make twenty enemies."

"I rarely make anybody happy in my business, so you're way ahead of me."

"But you protect people's lives. How can they be mad about that?"

"Easily."

"Weird."

He shrugged.

"You're also not much of a talker."

"If it helps, I've said more to you than to anybody in the last two hours."

"So you understand, right?" she asked, her tone taking on a hint of pleading. "You could let me hang around the events this weekend. I won't bother anybody, then I can find out—"

"No."

She looked astonished by his abrupt response. "No?"

"I appreciate the difficult position you're in, Ms. Lindsey, but I have a job, as well— One I'd like to keep." Though he had no idea why. "Stay away from the wedding events, and we'll get along just fine."

She seemed truly disappointed. "You won't help me?"

"I can't."

As he turned away, she laid her hand on his forearm. Shock and desire shot through him. *Damn.*

"You must have some sympathy for my cause," she said softly. "You waited awhile before confronting me. Why?"

"Curiosity and boredom."

She moved around him, standing close enough that their torsos nearly touched. "And are you still bored?"

She smelled amazing. Like vanilla and spice, comforting and warm. Like a scent from his childhood or his grandmother's kitchen.

He empathized with her wanting to save her business and reputation. He liked that she seemed to understand what he was thinking without him saying much, if anything. He appreciated her honesty and directness.

And he was crazy about those eyes.

"Are you planning to seduce me to your cause?" he asked, his heart picking up speed in hopeful anticipation.

Heat swam through her eyes for a second, then she stepped

back and let go of his arm. "No." She shook her head, as if clearing it. "No, I'm not."

Too bad.

Even as his libido surged with that thought, he dismissed it. He had a job to do. Didn't he always?

"Boss?" The crackling deep voice came from the walkie-talkie clipped to his belt.

"Yeah?" Wade answered, knowing his time with the lovely Tara Lindsey was truly about to come to an end.

"Code Lavender," Marco returned from the depths of the speaker.

Already? *Hell.* "I'll be right there." He returned the walkie-talkie to his belt and knew his reluctance to leave wasn't simply because of the mundane ridiculousness of his job.

"What's Code Lavender?" Tara asked.

"Drunk bridesmaid."

"I take it back, Mr. Cooper," she said with an amused smirk. "Your job is in much greater jeopardy than mine. Don't let me keep you from it."

"Saving people from themselves seems to have become my specialty," he muttered as he walked away.

He didn't look back at first. But then he remembered the sacrifices of his past had led to a present he wasn't all that crazy about and a future promising more of the same. This was all he had, all he'd ever have.

He'd already lost the love of his life. Why shouldn't he make time for something else for a change?

Stopping, he turned toward her. "Maybe we could have a drink at the bar later? One not on J. D. Maynard's tab."

"Sure," she said, the sarcasm clear. "Call me anytime."

Wade finally smiled. Along with blowing him off, she was apparently confident he had no idea how to get in touch with her.

She didn't know he was a first-rate investigator.

At least he used to be.

3

"YOU CAN'T HAVE ANY MORE crappy roast beef, Ms. Lindsey, but you can have me."

Tara moaned. She *really* wanted him. His broad, strong body hovered over hers. His raspy, commanding voice echoed in her ear. His blue-black hair glinted in the moonlight.

As his hand caressed her bare thigh, her body pulsed in response. Maybe this was moving too fast. Her ears rang.

Literally.

Dragging her way out of the dream, she groped for the phone on the bedside table. "Is the hotel on fire?"

"No," said a familiar and commanding voice.

Despite her sleep-deprived state, Tara shivered in delight. "Do you know what the hell time it is?"

"Two-fifteen."

Tara shot straight up in bed. "You're kidding," she said, though the bedside clock confirmed his response.

"You said call you anytime."

"That was sarcasm."

"I know. So how 'bout that drink?"

Struggling to shed the vestiges of sleep from her brain, she rubbed her temples. Maybe if he spent some time with her, he'd understand how badly losing this contract had damaged her business and her confidence. Maybe she could convince him to look the other way while she spied on Carla and her staff.

Besides, when was the last time a hot stranger had invited her anywhere?

"That's a really long pause," he said into the silence.

"Okay, fine. I'll meet you in the bar in fifteen minutes."

She dropped the phone in its cradle before either of them could change their minds.

She was, by nature, an impulsive person. A curse the French pastry chef at her mother's NYC restaurant had tried unsuccessfully to exorcise from her DNA at regular intervals over the years.

"Zee pastry is like a fragile child" he'd said at least a thousand times. "You must have patience, *mademoiselle*."

Yeah, yeah. In a minute.

With a little concealer, blush and mascara in place, and her mass of waves pinned on top of her head, she appeared in the bar only a couple of minutes over the promised time.

The entrance guard was gone as were the buffet tables, the somewhat disturbing steer-shaped ice sculpture and the paparazzis' wet dream throng of guests.

Wade Cooper, Security Chief, was sitting at the bar's far end with a cut crystal glass of amber liquid in front of him.

Dark and sexy, he was as hot as she remembered. Which, frankly, she would have thought impossible a few hours earlier. Plus, he'd piqued her curiosity. There was no way a guy like him had as his biggest ambition bouncer-bodyguard at a celebrity wedding.

What was his story?

"The lady would like a look at your wine list, Bobby," he said to the bartender as he pulled out the stool next to him.

Tara started to wave away the small, leather-bound book out of sheer stubbornness, but she was curious. "How could you possibly know I was going to order wine?"

He shrugged his broad shoulders—his seemingly favorite gesture. "You look like a wine woman."

"Uh-huh." *Curiouser and curiouser.* "What does a wine woman look like exactly?"

"You."

"Do I?"

She held his gaze a moment, but the smokiness in his eyes was as unreadable as ever. Certain she wasn't going to solve his puzzle anytime soon, she focused on the menu, then ordered a glass of pinot noir.

When the glass of deep red liquid was in front of her, she grasped the stem and lifted it in a toast. "To mind reading."

As she sipped, he eyed her skeptically. "You don't really think I read your mind, do you?"

"No." But he was very observant. Did she give off wine vibes? And what were those exactly? She wasn't sure she wanted to know. "How was the debauchery?"

"Controlled."

"That doesn't seem like the usual agenda for a bachelor or bachelorette party."

He ran the tip of his finger around the rim of his glass. "It is when I'm in charge of them."

With the finality of his tone and the awkward silence that followed, she sipped her wine. The balance of fruit and acidity was excellent, but she found herself struggling to appreciate the subtlety.

This was an odd date-drink invitation. He'd barely looked at her. His body was tense and his manner reserved. She'd gotten out of bed—and a pretty nice dream—at 2:15 a.m. for this?

"Do you want to know why I'm drinking whiskey?" he asked suddenly.

Where is this going? "Uh…sure."

"I needed it tonight."

Her alarm increased. What did she really know about this guy? "No kidding."

"I could barely focus on my job."

"Why's that?"

His gaze jumped to hers and held. "I thought about you."

"Oh." Should she tell him she dreamed about him? Probably not. Especially given the erotic nature of her dream. She didn't know him.

Though, somehow, she did.

He seemed alone, even surrounded by people.

"Is thinking about me a bad thing?" she asked, sensing it was.

"When I'm working it is. I've always been focused on my job." He sipped his whiskey. "Even this one."

Finally, a kernel of what lay behind that strong facade. "You don't like your job?"

"Yes. No." He shrugged yet again. "I used to like it more."

She'd have bet her best set of knives that he was a lifetime lawman. "What did you used to do?"

"Work for the Secret Service."

She choked on her wine. "As in the guys in suits and sunglasses who run beside the President's motorcade?"

He narrowed his eyes. "We do a bit more than that, but yes."

Though the revelation made perfect sense, she found herself wildly impressed. "Why don't you work there anymore?"

"I was part of an undercover operation to stop a counterfeiting ring. One of the suspects shot me in the thigh, shattering the bone. Afterward, I couldn't pass the physical to stay in the Service."

Tara's heart contracted. She didn't like picturing him lying in the hospital, alone—it would have to be alone—hurting and jobless. The nation's leader certainly deserved the smartest, strongest and quickest agents, but what little she knew about Wade Cooper suggested part of him had died knowing he no longer measured up.

Obviously guessing the direction of her thoughts, he angled

his body toward her and lifted one side of his mouth in a weak smile. "Sorry. I'm not a fan of self-pity. I should be grateful I can still work at all. You risked arrest to save your job."

"Not only my job," she felt compelled to point out, "my company. I have five full-time employees and twelve part-time servers, and most of them are struggling college students, so—"

He held up his hand. "I get it. I'm not going to have you arrested."

"But you're not going to let me in, either."

"I can't. I have an obligation to my employer, just like you have to your employees."

The barrier wouldn't discourage her, but she saw the futility in arguing. For the moment anyway. "We have career struggles in common, I guess."

"And Texas."

"I can definitely toast to Texas."

As their glasses clinked, the awkwardness flicked off and the chemistry from that first moment he'd confronted her was renewed.

Tara learned they'd both gone to the University of Texas and were devoted to Dallas Cowboys football. Wade had even played at UT, but at the time Tara had been involved with the indy music crowd and not sports, so she hadn't heard of his senior year, record-setting yardage.

They'd both left Austin to work in different cities—Wade in Washington and Tara in Manhattan—but had ended up back in the Texas capitol. Living in the same city, they'd eaten at many of the same restaurants, though they were the places Tara considered occasional junk food forays and Wade used as near staples.

"You're not going to keep that rock-hard body eating chicken fried steak at Joe's," Tara asserted.

"What do you know about my body?"

She let her gaze drift briefly over his broad chest and got a pretty good mental image of the muscled, swarthy skin beneath. Her mouth dry, she managed to respond with "I've got eyes."

He leaned toward her, and the scent of his spice-laden cologne mingled with the whiskey on his breath. "Anytime you want an up-close view, you're welcome."

Memories of her dream flitted through her mind. "We barely know each other."

And yet his compelling presence and the power of impulse mixed with a needy libido as if she'd dumped them all into a food processor.

"I should go. Thanks for the wine."

He grabbed her hand as she slid off the bar stool. "I didn't mean to run you off."

A spark of desire shot from her fingers to low in her belly. "You aren't. I just…" She made the mistake of looking into his handsome face and seeing a flame behind his smoky eyes. "You're very tempting."

"You, too."

The silence stretched for what seemed like minutes before he gave her hand a light squeeze. "I'll walk you to your door." He signed the check and escorted her toward the lobby. "I have to be up at six."

"Six? Surely the bridal party will sleep in." She didn't want to elaborate and say she'd heard the guests talking earlier about the dress and tux fittings scheduled for eleven the next morning. Or that she intended to be there.

"They probably will, but the fans and paparazzi won't. I found one guy last night who'd sneaked into the bar's walk-in fridge and planned to spend the night."

"Those things are airtight. He could have died in there."

"Didn't seem to concern him. He came out shivering and mumbling, 'G-got to h-have the sh-shot.' It was pitiful."

They fell back into an easy conversational rhythm, as if the enticing invitation and her immediate retreat had never occurred. Tara appreciated the switch, though she doubted any amount of reflection would help her explain her sudden and fascinating attraction to a man she hadn't known existed twelve hours ago.

Maybe when they got back home they could have dinner, an actual date or something, and see what happened. Right now, she needed to focus on saving her business, and since Wade had made it clear they were on opposite sides of her method to accomplish that, it was best if they kept their distance.

As they headed down the hall toward her room, she halted suddenly. "Hang on. How did you know what room I'm in?"

"I called earlier, remember?"

"But I'm not registered under my name."

"You used your mother's. Not a big leap for an ace investigator like me. Especially since I have full access to the resort's guest records."

"When I blew you off earlier, I was counting on you not being able to find me."

"I know."

"You're pretty sneaky," she decided as they resumed walking down the hall.

"Coming from you I consider that a compliment. Besides, I have the feeling I'll need every advantage with you."

Did he suspect she wasn't giving up her quest? Did he realize that, even now, she'd already started Phase II?

Probably, but she wasn't about to ask. She was a lousy liar, and she didn't need guilt piled on top of carnal frustration and sleep deprivation.

"Thanks again for the drink," she said when they reached her room. "Maybe when we get back home, I could make you dinner sometime?"

He leaned against the wall next to her door. "Not chicken fried steak, I guess."

"How about a two-inch-thick T-bone?"

"Talk about tempting."

She grinned. "So? You'll call me next week?"

"Sure."

She held out her hand. "I expect we won't see much of each other this weekend, so it was nice meeting you. I'm sure it'll be a lovely wedding."

He stared at her outstretched hand, then took it and pulled her against his chest. "Don't forget the cupcakes. At our dinner, I mean."

"You only get those if you tell me how you knew I wasn't invited to the party."

"I remember the deal." His gaze roved her face, dropping briefly to her lips. "You don't have to hide behind your mother's name, you know."

"I'm aware of that."

"It's okay to stand on your own."

She lifted her chin. "For you, too."

After a slight hesitation, he bobbed his head in acknowledgment. Then, brushing his warm lips across her cheek, he was gone.

4

"THESE CRAB THINGS ARE amazing," Holly Addison remarked to her collection of bridesmaids as she shoved another one in her mouth.

"I know," the blonde on her left answered, reaching toward the silver platter for another. "If I keep eating these, I'll never fit into that dress."

"Really, Holly, darling," a six-foot-tall woman with artfully waved brown hair said. Standing on a pedestal in a semicircle of mirrors, she sucked in her stomach as an assistant tried to zip her dress. "Couldn't you have found a more forgiving fabric than satin?"

"You're the one who drank four margaritas last night, *darling*," Holly returned, followed by a benign smile.

Wearing a blond wig and her chef's coat while pretending to straighten the flower arrangement on the small buffet table, Tara beamed as she listened to the bride's and her attendants' praise of the snacks on display.

Last night, after leaving Wade to handle the Code Lavender crisis, she'd made her way to the hotel's kitchen, where she'd charmed the staff and learned Carla's Posh Events team was providing hors d'oeuvres to the wedding party during their final tux and dress fittings. Andre, the resort's pastry chef, was wildly put out by both Carla's high-handed manner and her refusal to use any local specialties for her spread.

She'd further demanded "complete privacy" to make her precious tidbits out of fear Andre and his staff would steal her valuable recipes.

With his culinary heritage and his pride bruised, Andre had been an easy recruit to Tara's plan to make her own spread and serve it before Carla's staff arrived at the dress shop.

After tasting the offerings last night, she and Andre were confident of winning the head-to-head battle, and then she'd have proof—in her own mind as well as testimony from the bride—of her culinary superiority. With that knowledge, she planned to confront J. D. Maynard and ask him why she'd been rejected.

Ideally he'd tell her why he'd chosen Posh Events, then, admiring Tara's spunk as well as her food, he'd recommend her to his rich friends, thereby saving her business.

See, I'm already standing on my own, Agent Cooper.

"My favorite is this pastry thing," another woman commented, scooping up one of the desserts artfully placed in a scalloped-edged paper cup. "I can't place the fruit, though."

"It's guava," Tara offered with a polite smile. "The dish is called guava duff, a traditional Bahamian dessert, and made especially for you ladies by the staff at the resort."

During the *mmms* and *oohs* that followed, Tara set out the last of her and Andre's selections, then withdrew to the shop's storeroom. She'd cut her timing close to the expected arrival of Carla and her staff to hear the ladies' reactions, but she needed to get into her secluded position before she was recognized by her rival.

No sooner had she stepped past the curtain separating the luxurious shop from its cluttered back room than an iron grip captured her arm.

Looking at her captor to identify him wasn't necessary, but compelled to do so anyway, she stared into the angry face of Wade Cooper.

"Well, well, Ms. Lindsey, when did you become a brides-maid?"

"Cute. I couldn't fit in one of those tummy-sucking tube dresses if my life depended on it." Seeing little point in subter-fuge, she dragged off the wig. "I should have known the disguise wouldn't fly, even for that dunce you put by the front door this morning."

"I knew you were up to something last night."

Tara fought against a pout. "I figured. That's why I wore the wig."

"Didn't do you much good. I'd recognize those eyes any-where."

The intensity behind his eyes was well on display itself. Point-ing that out at the moment, however, seemed unwise. Besides, she had heat of her own. "Is that why you invited me for a drink last night—to uncover my dastardly plan?"

For the first time since she'd met him, he looked surprised. "No."

"You just felt the need for a drink at two-fifteen in the morn-ing."

"Yes."

"And you didn't want to drink alone."

"I wanted to be with *you*."

The anger and disappointment on his face said far more than his sharp tone. "You don't now," she said as she stepped back.

She should have been honest with him last night, she real-ized. She should have found a way to convince him that her plan wasn't to make his job more difficult, or to disrupt the Maynard's privacy. "I fed your clients for free, and they're happy," she said, still too annoyed to apologize. "Why aren't you?"

"They—" he flung his hand in the direction of the shop's interior "—are not my clients. J. D. Maynard is."

"You need some crab cakes," Tara said, turning from his glowering face. "And definitely a guava duff."

He snagged her hand and dragged her to his side. "Stay."

Tara wrenched herself from his grasp. "Look, you're really hot and interesting, and I like you, but I'm not big on manhandling, so don't—"

He yanked her back against him and covered her mouth with his huge hand. "That's your competition coming through the back door," he whispered in her ear.

The protest that had risen to her lips died. She stilled, and Wade's body relaxed, as well. He removed his hand from her mouth, but kept her tucked against him, his hand braced against her stomach.

As she heard Carla's fake-but-peppy greeting to the bridal party, she was distinctly aware of Wade's heart beating firmly against her back.

His scent and warmth washed over her like a wave of comforting strength. He might not be fully with her, but he wasn't against her. Did that mean they were on opposite sides or somewhere in the middle of the chasm?

She was here to save her business—the most important thing in her life. Yet she realized she'd fallen into a much deeper pool, and treading water wasn't likely possible for much longer.

WADE CLOSED HIS EYES AND kept his body absolutely still.

He fought to remember his sniper training. The desire for relaxation, yet the need for watchfulness. *No sudden moves. Let them come to you.*

But the impression of Tara's body against his was the only thing he could feel.

At least his hearing still worked.

The sound of movement in the main part of the shop floated to him. The catering staff was laying out their platters and confused by the ones already present.

"Your assistant brought them a while back," one of the women said. "The blond girl."

"Did she?" an aggressive voice responded.

"Hey, don't take that" was heard next.

"But we have fresh spinach canapés." The aggressive voice was more placating, but not by much.

"Yay for you," said the first voice. "But take that platter of crab puffs, and I'm going to hurt you."

Tara glanced back at Wade. "Told you they liked my food," she whispered.

"I'm sure they do," Wade responded. "But then you aren't up against much competition."

"How do you—"

He pressed his palm against her stomach, sending a fresh wave of need careening through his body. "Listen."

He closed his eyes to force himself to do the same.

The conversation shifted away from the food. They heard complaints about the dress—too tight, too shiny. That was coupled with a few bawdy comments about the groom, then his groomsmen, then his father, who was apparently known for a big bank account, multiple wives and small body parts.

"No comment is worse than a complaint," Tara said, keeping her voice low.

"I doubt J. D. Sr. would agree."

She lightly jabbed her elbow against his ribs. "I was talking about the food."

"A good meal isn't going to pump up J.D.'s shriveled ego."

"Sex. Is that all men think about?"

Since she'd turned and was presently standing in the intimate circle of his arms, Wade didn't see how he could deny the obvious. "Really good food is a close second."

"Yippee." She rolled her eyes. "Runner-up. Don't I love that position?"

Nothing about Tara Lindsey was second best. The fact that she could even consider casting herself in that role bothered him way more than it probably should. As she'd pointed out the night before, they barely knew each other.

But the disappointment in their life's work, after giving everything they had, was common ground. Their sacrifices had led absolutely nowhere. Sure, they were on their own, but they were failing.

Him in purpose; her in finances.

Before he could say any of that, though, she rolled on.

"I don't see what the big deal is by me coming here." Her vivid blue eyes narrowed. "I'm not bothering anybody."

"You're doing a damn good job of distracting me."

She flicked her gaze to her hand, lying palm down against his chest. "I know what you mean."

Loyalties warred inside him. Clearly Tara had been shafted, but J.D. had hired her rival. Wade didn't necessarily like his job, respect his employer or agree with him, but protecting his interests was essential. If the client wanted bad food along with uninvited photographers in restraints, that's what he got.

A small voice reminded Wade that he didn't always follow a protectee's orders. If there was suspected or eminent danger, all orders were mute.

But he wasn't in the world of life-or-death decisions anymore.

He saved drunk bridesmaids from the effects of top-shelf margaritas.

And yet compromising his professionalism wasn't in his DNA. No matter how much he respected and wanted Tara, they weren't going to walk side by side this weekend.

"I think my backup Paul can handle bad spinach canapés," he said finally. "Let's talk outside."

After slipping through the back door, he faced Tara in the bright tropical sunshine. Her dark hair was clipped back to conceal it beneath the blond wig, but she immediately leaned her head back and thrust her fingers through the waves, scattering pins and sending his need for her soaring.

Still, he did the difficult thing. Wasn't that what he was paid for? Trained for? "We're on opposite sides of this."

Her gaze jumped to his. "Are we?"

"Yes."

"I don't want to be."

"Me, either."

"So why are we?"

"Because I have a job to do, and you don't respect the boundaries I've set."

"I'm trying to save my business," she snapped.

"I'm trying to do my job."

Her face flushed deep red, and he was pretty certain it wasn't because of the heat.

"Opposite sides," he repeated.

"Fine." She turned, presumably to leave, but ground to a halt after only two steps and the words they both heard a short distance away.

"Look, J.D., I've made a lot of sacrifices to make this wedding special for Junior."

Tara glanced back at Wade and mouthed *Carla*.

Having eavesdropped on more than a few conversations in his career, Wade moved to Tara's side, took her by the arm and pulled her next to the building. Carla and Maynard Sr. were around the corner, near the entrance.

"I paid you to make it special," J.D. returned angrily. "And I've heard a lot of grumbling about your food. With the bills I'm paying, I oughta be getting better."

"You're getting *exactly* what you're paying for," Carla returned, her tone unyielding.

A door slam followed this statement.

Tara turned toward Wade. "Well, now, wasn't that interesting?"

5

"CLIENTS OFTEN DISAGREE with vendors."

Though Tara knew Wade's words to be absolutely true—having been on the losing end of an irrational and disgruntled client a few times—she didn't think the argument was quite so insignificant. "But vendors never talk back. The client is always right."

"To you, maybe. That Carla chick doesn't seem the type to apologize too often."

But Maynard Sr. was one of the richest men in Texas. Why would she be dumb enough to piss him off? "Earlier you said there wasn't much competition between me and Carla. What did you mean?"

"There *is* no competition."

"Apparently there is. I'm losing contracts to her."

"Wouldn't be the first mistake Maynard made. I tasted her food last night. And I did eat a crab cake. No contest."

"So isn't it hard to believe she can be rude, expensive, serve crappy food *and* still be stealing my best customers?"

Wade's expression was speculative. "Good point."

Tara bit her lip. "The question is, how is she doing it?"

"Do you really think Paul is a dunce?"

Oh, so Mr. Security Chief wasn't going to help her save her business, but he wanted advice on his. She patted his shoulder in what she sincerely hoped was a condescending gesture. "The door he was guarding? I breezed through it with food on a silver tray, chef's jacket and a laminated ID tag I made at Walgreens last week."

Before walking away she had the pleasure of seeing him wince.

"Have fun during the excursions this afternoon," she added. "Water-skiing, scuba diving and snorkeling, I hear. I'm only sorry I can't witness you keeping law and order, bare-chested and wearing only a bathing suit. I wonder which trashy tabloid reporter will be the first to buzz the island in a helicopter?"

"Hang on," he shouted after her. "How did you know about the excursions?"

Tara didn't answer. She smiled and kept walking.

BY DINNERTIME, TARA'S amusement had long since faded.

She'd skulked around the beach and resort all afternoon and hadn't seen hide nor hair of J. D. Maynard Sr. Now that she knew her food was superior, she had to find out where she'd gone wrong. How was she supposed to confront the man, charm him and win future business if she couldn't even find him?

But then, there was always the chance she'd get to him by admitting they were her surreptitious—but free—snack offerings at the dress shop, and he'd call the intimidating Wade Cooper, who'd then either have her arrested or tossed off the island entirely.

Not a promising path to success.

Without Maynard to charm, she'd instead listened in on dozens of conversations, hoping for more hints about the schedule later that night and the wedding the next day, and concluded there was some sort of party, but she had no idea where.

"It's probably best to leave the investigating to the professionals," she muttered as, exhausted, she entered her room a few minutes after five.

"I couldn't agree more."

Lounging in the desk chair was none other than Chief Cooper himself.

"What the hell are you doing?" she demanded, adva
toward him. "How did you get in?"

He flipped his hand to show her a key card.

"Look, buddy, that's going too far," she said, snatchi
plastic from his hand. "This is my room. You can't inva o
privacy like this."

Unruffled, he simply stared at her. "You're not just a sus
party crasher, you're a confessed one."

"You're an ass. And you're probably some weirdo who
to go through women's underwear drawers."

Of course she knew he wasn't, since she'd also spe
afternoon using her cell phone to check out his Secret Se
story. "Treasury Agent a True Hero" was her favorite hea

His smoky eyes churned with promise. "I generally get
to see underwear on an actual woman."

Bracing her hand on the desk, she leaned close to him_
just bet you do."

The proximity sent the emotion that had started as a
zipping in a new, more carnal direction. Maybe it was her fi
tration finally breaking free, maybe it was chemistry, may i
was him.

In the next breath, her lips were fused with his.

He pulled her into his lap, his hands roaming up her bac
his tongue invaded her mouth. She sighed into him as her a
curled around his neck. He was certainly as strong and haro
she'd imagined, but seductive, as well. He knew how to kiss
put his whole focus into the act.

Her heart pounded; her breathing grew labored. And de e
wound itself around her, binding her to him like a rope.

When the kiss finally broke, they stared at each other, pant
and dazed, knowing a line had been crossed from which t
weren't going to retreat.

Still, she felt self-conscious, having attacked the man a
she were both desperate and lonely—which, basically, she w
But she needed cash more than a man.

Didn't she?

She sat up, and he let his hands fall to the chair's armrest. "Sorry."

"Happy to be here for you."

"It's been a long day," she offered, searching for some common ground.

"Did *you* pull a photographer out of the ocean who'd used a faulty bungee cord to lash himself to the side of a speedboat in an effort to get an exclusive shot of Holly Addison in her wedding bikini?"

"Ah, no."

"Then I win the crappy day prize."

"I guess you do." She angled her head. "Wedding bikini?"

"White, obviously. With a lace and crystal train attached to the back like a fish tail. Or maybe a fish veil. Custom-made by some Paris designer, who apparently failed to notice the fabric became transparent when it got wet."

"So other than drowning paparazzi, you watched over a bunch of scantily clad starlets all day. 'Scuse me, but that doesn't sound so bad—at least from your point of view."

For the first time since she'd met him, his lips broke into a broad smile. "There are some excellent plastic surgeons and personal trainers in Beverly Hills, and their specialty seems to be boobs and butts."

"I'll bet."

"I saw you spying from the beach. Hot blue bikini. You spend some time at the gym yourself."

"With my proximity to rich food, regular exercise is pretty much a necessity." And how nice he'd noticed. Especially surrounded by those perfect Hollywood chicks. Maybe he— "Hold on, how did you see me? I never saw you."

"Binoculars."

"That's a bit…unnerving."

"A tool necessary for the job. Kind of like your need for a whisk."

"Funny, I don't see the correlation at all. If you want to see me in my bikini, you might try asking." She narrowed her eyes. "Kind of like entering my room."

"Okay. But catching you in the binocular sights was an accident the first time." He scooped a stack of folded papers off the desk. "And I only came by to bring you this. As you'll see, it's not something I'm comfortable handing over in public. I was writing you a note when you came in."

Looking down at the paper, she noticed the bold scrawl of the words *Tara, I thought you might…* But as she started to flip open the stack, she recalled a particularly interesting part of his confession. "The first time?"

His gray eyes gleamed. "I liked looking at you. I kept coming back."

Her whole body went hot. "Did you? What about all those nosy reporters lurking around? Didn't you want to keep an eye on them?"

"Except for bungee cord guy, they went with helicopters—nice call on that, by the way."

"I've catered for celebrities, rich folks, demanding crazy people and the political elite. I've seen some strange stuff in the name of party crashing."

"Which is why you knew what to do this weekend."

"Apparently I don't." She dropped the stack of paper in her lap, then covered his hands with hers and leaned closer. "I keep getting caught."

"Understandable. I'm pursuing you pretty hard."

"Are you?"

His gaze roved her face, then focused on her lips. "It's a little hard to keep my balance, but yeah."

She understood his meaning. They had obligations to their jobs that weren't meshing with their desire for each other. Like dieters licking chocolate off their fingers, they couldn't seem to find the willpower to say no.

When he brought one hand up to cup her cheek, she melted into him like a gooey treat. She gave herself over to a kiss that was more tender than she'd expected, more needy than simple stress relief. He explored her mouth as if he planned to spend all day doing so.

The faint scent of coconut-laden sunscreen as well as sea air wafted from his skin, enveloping her in a forbidden island fantasy and exotic sensations. His arms, though banded around her like steel, held her with exquisite care.

She had no idea what they were doing, plastered together like magnets. But she knew she was glad he'd come, and she didn't want to let him go.

Parting, she let her forehead rest against his. "This is crazy."

"Then sign me up for the loony bin."

"Done." Smiling, she pressed another kiss to his lips. "I guess you have to go back to work." A fact she regretted more than she expected.

He lifted the stack of paper he'd brought. "See for yourself."

Straightening, she unfolded the packet. Her shocked gaze jumped to his. "This is the wedding events schedule."

"It is."

Her heart pounded as hard as when he'd kissed her the first time. "Why?"

"You got the shaft with the catering. I stand for truth and justice and all that jazz. At least I used to."

"Truth and justice and all that jazz?"

"It's supposed to mean something—not only for the rich and famous, but everybody. And especially you, particularly when I have something to say about it."

His concern warmed her heart. He'd built a bridge between their opposing sides, and she was more interested than ever in finding out where their paths might meet.

She noted both a rehearsal dinner for family and the wedding party and a nightclub party for everybody else were taking place during the next few hours. The air leaked from the balloon of hope of satisfying her desire. "It looks like you're going to be busy tonight."

"I could bring up leftovers from the dinner."

"Is this a meal Carla's cooking?"

"Based on the resentful kitchen staff, I'd say so."

"Then no, thanks. But I could call room service—the resentful kitchen staff does know a culinary thing or two. Maybe we could have a late dinner?"

"I'll bring the wine," he agreed immediately.

With a seemingly effortless move, he rose from the chair with her in his arms. She could really get used to this.

At the door, he set her down, then pressed his lips briefly to hers. "I'll see you around nine—after the dinner and before things get out of control at the nightclub. Then I'll help you find Maynard Sr. He's really the only one who can answer your questions about losing the wedding contract."

"Okay." Her heart resumed its excited pounding. The possibility of having a heart-to-heart with a billionaire who might become a future client wasn't the only cause. After all, all work and no play made for a cranky—if financially solvent—caterer.

Wade paused with his hand on the door. "Oh, and something squirrelly's going on with that Carla chick."

Spoken like a true Texan. "She got her cooking lessons from the Academy of Tasteless Hoes?"

He grinned, and she wondered how she'd ever had a hard time picturing a smile on his face. "Probably. And her financials are way off base for a caterer."

"How do you know anything about her financial status?"

He simply raised his eyebrows.

"Right. You have access to information I don't."

"I've got a hunch."

"What—"

He held up his hand. "Let me see where it goes. I have to deal with this rehearsal dinner, then we'll talk."

"Just talk?"

He brushed his lips across her cheek. "And eat. Don't forget room service."

6

WADE LISTENED TO THE maid of honor droning on with her postdinner toast to the bride and resisted the urge to check his watch.

Again.

Was the woman going for some kind of record? Where was the loud and impatient orchestra, playing her offstage before she'd started listing the reasons Holly Addison had played a critical role in the life of her Jack Russell terrier?

I've got a hot woman and a hot meal waiting for me upstairs. Lift the damn glass already!

As was expected by his role in this little drama, though, he exposed none of these thoughts. He scanned the room for anybody who didn't belong. He made note of Paul's intent watchfulness at the door separating the rehearsal dinner party from the rest of the restaurant. After yesterday's lack of attention, and Wade's threat to send his ass home without his full paycheck, he'd obviously decided to take his job more seriously.

He saw Tara's competition, Carla Castalono, watching the proceedings from the back corner of the room, a smug smile on her face. As far as he could tell, she hadn't lifted a finger to help either her staff or the resort's pull off the multicourse dinner.

Instead, she'd chosen to fawn over the bride and groom, keeping their wine and champagne glasses filled.

Based on the guests' reaction to the bland-looking meal, he imagined the booze was appreciated.

A prickle at the back of his neck reminded him of his suspicion that something was off at Posh Events.

And it wasn't only the lousy food.

Finally, finally, the maid of honor lifted her fluted glass, and the toast was done. She then tossed back the contents and ended the ordeal with a blessedly brief and enthusiastic, "Let's party!"

Keeping an outward calm but inwardly jumping for joy, Wade spoke to Marco, his second-in-command, gave Paul a warning glare, then slid from the room. His lieutenants could handle a couple of hours on their own.

He fought the urge to run straight to the elevator and instead dived into the hotel gift shop for wine, flowers and condoms. *You have to think positive to get positive results,* his coach at UT used to preach. A much sager—and shorter—toast to a successful life than the one he'd just heard.

When he arrived at Tara's door, he used every ounce of crisis-management training and experience he possessed to calm his pulse and remind himself that he'd come a long way since he'd gotten his first girl in the back of his Chevy.

Which did him no good when Tara opened the door and faced him wearing a white halter-top sundress and a sultry smile of welcome.

Balancing the wine and flowers in one arm, he wrapped the other around her waist and backed her into the room. She threw her arms around his neck and pulled him toward the bed. They fell on their sides onto the comforter, her leg wrapped around his hip.

The flowers and wine bottle tumbled, forgotten, to the floor. He slid his hands down her back and cupped her butt, pressing her center against his erection. The contact felt so good, so delightfully torturous, he groaned.

She responded by shoving off his jacket, then ripping open his shirt, which got stuck on his shoulder holster. But with a few shrugs and a released fastener, she was quickly gliding her hands over his skin. "You're on fire. You're probably sunburned."

"Just hot."

Her gaze roved his face, then his bare chest. "You are indeed."

Smiling, he moved his mouth down the silky curve of her throat and untied the halter. She wore nothing beneath, and he took almost no time to flick his tongue across her distended nipple.

She arched her back, pressing herself into him, silently asking for more.

He'd have given her the planet, the stars and moon in that moment. With only the faint bedside light casting a glow, she looked like a spirit from another world, her delicate curves calling to his instincts, sending him spiraling into the whirlpool of desire.

He pushed the dress and her satin white panties down her hips and off the end of the bed while she unbuttoned his pants. When her hand wrapped confidently around his erection, he thought he stopped breathing.

When she slid her hand down, then up again, he knew he had.

Gritting his teeth against exploding, he slid his fingers between her legs. The wet heat spiked his lust, but the breathless, lingering kiss she placed at the base of his throat reminded him that his needs weren't his first priority.

He stroked her, parting her soft flesh and finding the button that would drive her to the edge with him.

In response, she squeezed his erection.

"Back pocket," he croaked.

She needed no further direction. Finding the condom, she

tore the foil with her teeth and rolled on the protection. As he moved between her thighs, her eyes were glazed with hunger, but she moved her fingers across his cheek in a whisper touch as if savoring the moment just before they became one.

His heart jumped, and he realized in an instant that this wasn't a weekend fling.

At least not for him.

Unable to deny the hunger any longer, he pressed inside her body, sighing with relief when he drove in fully. Her breathing became choppy. She dropped her hands and clutched the comforter as she drove her hips up to meet his.

She was through with tender strokes. She needed satisfaction. And now.

Rocking his hips, he set a rhythm of relief rather than seduction. Tenderness could follow, but now their bodies demanded release. She bowed her neck and back as she braced her palms against his chest and drove her hips up to meet his.

Her fingers danced in a tremble the instant before she came. Her inner walls squeezed him, and he let his own satisfaction soar. The pumps and waves of pleasure seemed to go on endlessly, and when it was reduced to intermittent quivers, he gathered her close and held her against his hammering heart, careful to collapse on his side and keep his weight off her.

For the first time since being forced to leave the Service, he felt a crazy flutter in his heart that might have been happiness.

THEY BROUGHT THE ROOM service tray into bed.

Tara had gone for a menu she knew would please a Texan, while including some local Caribbean specialties. The T-bone steak and a spicy conch chowder were the highlights.

As well as her feeding bites to a naked and appreciative Wade Cooper.

"Did you like playing football?" she asked.

"I liked being part of a team."

Propped beside her against the headboard, his wide shoulders and muscled chest made her mouth water more than the food. And that was saying something because the resort staff knew how to make chowder. "And you liked the Secret Service for the same reason?"

"Yeah. Plus I liked making a difference. The work we did mattered. Now I'm just a hired gun. Who doesn't even get to use his gun anymore."

"What you're doing now matters." She shoved another bite of chowder into his mouth as he started to protest. "Forget it's a Texas billionaire's son and a Hollywood A-list actress. It's Holly and J.D.'s wedding. The most important day of their lives. And you're making it special."

"Is that what you tell yourself when you cash the check from a particularly difficult client?"

"No. Then I say, 'Please, don't let this bounce.' You saved that photographer today, remember? That's pretty damn cool."

Wade sipped from his wineglass. "It's a dubious honor to save somebody that ambitiously stupid."

"Maybe he has a wife and four kids in Oxnard to support. Don't be such a cynic. Tomorrow's spa day before the wedding. I think you should take an hour break for a relaxing massage."

His gray eyes sparked with interest. "Are you the masseuse?"

The image of a candlelit room and her running her oiled hands over his muscled back flashed through her mind. "We could insert that activity into the schedule."

"Provided I haven't completely screwed up by leaving my crew on their own tonight."

"They're undoubtedly lost without their fearless leader. I should probably feel guilty."

"But you don't."

"Nope." She fed him another bite of chowder. "What was it like risking your life for the President?"

"Challenging."

"Did you get to use your gun a lot then?"

"Sure. But then the stakes were a lot higher. I haven't fired my weapon on the job in two years."

"But that's a good thing. You're scaring away all the really bad bad guys before they have a chance to strike."

"My most exciting project over the last year was on a pop star's concert tour."

"Sounds pretty dangerous to me. Some of those superfans can get pretty crazy."

Bafflement flooded his face. "Why are you determined to cast me in the role of hero?"

"If the cape fits…" She trailed the tip of her finger down his chest. "And I can personally testify that you'd look smokin' hot in brightly colored spandex."

After setting his glass on the nightstand, he slid his hand around the back of her head and pulled her close. "You do revolutionary things for a hotel robe. Though I think this particular one would look even better on the floor."

Her heart rate picked up its pace. The impulse to toss aside responsibility and indulge herself in the best kind of pampering was close to irresistible. "I thought you had to go back to work."

"I do, and I know you want to talk to Maynard." He drew his thumb across her bottom lip. "But the party has to end sometime."

"So after business…"

"Pleasure."

In answer, she pressed her lips to his. They'd known each other barely twenty-four hours and yet she felt closer to him than any man she'd dated in the past several years. She admired his dedication—as well as his body—and understood his need for a constant challenge.

Was this thing with them a reaction to frustration with their careers? Once the weekend was behind them and the balmy breezes subsided, would their chemistry fade? Or even disappear altogether?

They dragged themselves from the intimate confines of the bed, then dressed, though she eventually had to retreat to the bathroom because he kept trying to remove everything she put on.

Walking from the room, they linked hands. Their connection was about to be suspended. Security chief versus party crasher.

She dreaded going back to opposite camps, even if only for appearances.

At the door, he turned and his gaze locked with hers. "I *am* a cynic. I'm going through the motions of my job because I don't know anything else. And I'm pissed off I can't do what I love anymore. But I've smiled more in the last twenty-four hours than I have in the last twenty-four months." He pulled her close and added in a whisper, "Because of you."

Then again, maybe the balmy breezes were a beginning.

7

TARA HAD PROMISED HERSELF she wasn't going to eat anything at the nightclub party.

There were, of course, the ethics of eating something she hadn't been invited to sample, which was technically stealing. This was further complicated by her lover-of-less-than-an-hour-ago being in charge of keeping people like her behind the velvet rope—and there literally was a velvet rope. Purple, to match the bridesmaids' dresses. And lastly, but no less importantly, she wasn't keen on consuming anything Carla's crowd had whipped up.

But chocolate fountains rocked!

And they were apparently the one thing Carla couldn't make tasteless and boring. Maybe that's how she stole her clients.

She'd have to remember to ask Maynard if that particular carrot had been dangled when Carla had given her proposal for the wedding.

Though now that Tara was about to meet the powerful cattle rancher, she found her stomach churning. Either nerves or an overdose of chocolate were no doubt to blame.

Either way, she was reluctant to move from her viewing spot at the end of the long, curved bar trimmed in neon blue lights. The nightclub's DJ had the glittery crowd bumping and grinding to pulsing hot music. The bartenders' talent for mixology and the dessert fountains kept the partygoers from caring about the other boring culinary offerings.

And then there was Wade…prowling the room like a restless shadow and looking for trouble.

Sighing, Tara propped her chin on her fist and tracked him with her gaze. He really was dreamy. She could happily spend the next several hours, maybe even days, just watching his hunky body move. For the first time in years, her business wasn't her greatest priority.

She wanted him as much as solvency.

"Hey, honey. Are you Tara?"

Tara turned toward the male voice and found herself face-to-face with J. D. Maynard Sr.

Despite the tropical heat, he wore a long-sleeved white dress shirt, jeans, cowboy boots and a well-worn brown Stetson. His single nod to island life was an orange hibiscus tucked inside the band. "Texas Vacations in the Caribbean" would be the caption in the gossip mags.

She swallowed her jitters and held out her hand, which he shook as he slid onto the stool next to her. "I'm Tara. I guess Wade told you why I'm here."

Grinning, Maynard lifted his hand in the bartender's direction. "Nope, he just told me a hot brunette wanted to talk to me and told me where to find you." He winked. "My current wife is a brunette."

"The current one?" Clearly the rumor about Maynard's diminished physical attributes wasn't true. "How many have their been?"

"Four." Thankfully he turned away to look at the dancers, including his son, who were having the time of their lives, so he didn't see Tara's jaw drop. "Hope Junior has better luck. Who knows, though? Those Hollywood types are kinda flighty."

"Holly seems like a sensible girl, and she's totally devoted to J.D."

Maynard angled his head as the bartender set a glass of whiskey over ice in front of him. "You a friend of theirs? I know we haven't met. I'd remember those beautiful blue eyes."

"Oh, well, thanks." She'd expected a bit more formality, or even suspicion from the billionaire rancher née oil executive, and wasn't exactly sure how to tell him she wasn't supposed to be there at all. "Actually, I'm not one of the guests."

Maynard looked confused. "But Wade keeps real close tabs on all the guests. I asked him to. I can't have Junior's big day full of more reporters than friends."

Tara nodded. "I'm not a reporter. I'm a caterer. A few months ago, I met with your assistant to tell her about my menus for the wedding. I spent weeks on the proposal. I planned on local ingredients and dishes, while realizing a rancher's need for high-quality beef and also adding vegetarian options for the West Coast crowd. In short, I thought I had everything covered. At the tasting, your people seemed thrilled, but I didn't get the contract." She closed her eyes briefly. "My business is in serious trouble, Mr. Maynard. I've lost a lot of clients to Posh Events. I need to know why. I need to know what I'm doing wrong, or me and my staff will be looking for new jobs. So I'm crashing your son's wedding to spy on my competition."

To her surprise, Maynard didn't order her out of his party or even call Wade. He hunched over his cocktail glass. "You the one whose mom has that TV show?"

How did he know that? "Yes."

Looking suddenly deflated, he took a gulp of whiskey. "My assistant wanted to hire you. She went on and on about how great your food was and how enthusiastic and competent you were. Plus, she thought Holly would love bragging to her friends about a celebrity chef's daughter catering her wedding."

"But you didn't think so?" Tara had been around enough high-powered executives to know they didn't like decisions shoved down their throat. "Maybe she pushed too hard?"

"I—" His gaze cut to hers, then jumped away. "I had bigger concerns than cakes and crab puffs."

"I'm sure you did, and I'm sorry to confront you like this. I don't like admitting it, Mr. Maynard, but I'm desperate. You're a successful businessman. You know being one takes planning, attention to detail and great sacrifice. I just want to know what I'm doing wrong."

"I wish I could help you." He rose from his bar stool. "Have a drink on me and enjoy the wedding tomorrow. I officially invite you."

She laid her hand on his arm, stopping his retreat. "I don't want an invitation. I want an explanation."

He brought the back of her hand to his lips. "You're not getting one, honey. Sorry."

"Problem, Mr. Maynard?"

Tara was never so upset to hear Wade's deep voice than in that moment.

Maynard was about to sail off—though she still had no idea why he'd clammed up so abruptly—and Wade would demand she tell him everything they'd talked about. She'd look into that commanding face and spill every word. Then, like a hero, Wade would defend her to Maynard. He'd get fired, and Maynard would tell all his influential friends not to use that so-in-so Wade Cooper for their security.

She saw the whole, terrible scene like a movie reel on fast-forward.

"No problem," Maynard said to his security chief. "Give Tara whatever she wants. I'm going back to the party."

Wade's gaze slid to Tara.

She tried to erase any expression from her face, but she didn't expect to succeed. Wade had been trained to sense even the slightest hint of trouble; she doubted he'd fail to see a problem now.

Wade wrapped his hand around his employer's arm and guided—maybe even forced—him back to his seat. "Stay for another drink, sir. I have something relevant to say."

"Wade, please," Tara began, only to have him silence her with one glare of those sober gray eyes.

Knowing what was coming, and dreading the role she'd played in ruining everything, she nevertheless fell in love.

Wade was going to sacrifice himself for her, just as he'd done for years in Washington. Her cause was much less important, but she knew that wouldn't matter to him.

He was doing his job and standing between her and the bullet.

"I'D LIKE TO EXPLAIN ABOUT Clive Anderson," Wade said, standing between his lover and his boss.

There was an almost comical pause where the fierce annoyance on both Tara's and Maynard's faces turned to confusion.

Maynard recovered first and attempted to stand. "I don't know what you're up to, Cooper, but I'm paying for this party, and I'd like to enjoy it."

Wade laid his hand on his boss's shoulder to keep him in place. "I'd like to explain about Clive Anderson," he repeated.

"I can handle this, Wade. You don't need to defend me." Tara's eyes widened like saucers. "You really shouldn't."

"Clive Anderson," Wade went on as if he hadn't heard her protest, "is a sleazy, small-time private investigator with a serious gambling problem. He's currently keeping his bookies at bay with supposed gainful employment at Posh Events."

"Wade, you have to stop—" Tara stopped on her own as his words apparently penetrated that gorgeous, stubborn head of hers. "Why would a caterer need a P.I.?"

"Exactly the question I asked myself." He shifted his attention to Maynard. "Particularly one who specializes in blackmail."

"Blackmail?" Tara echoed. "Some P.I. with a gambling problem has forced Carla to hire him to help her cater?" She shook her head ruefully. "Really, Wade, I appreciate you trying to help, but doesn't that seem a little—"

"Carla isn't the blackmail victim," Wade said, his glare locked on Maynard's face.

After a long pause, Maynard's bony shoulders slumped. "Fine. Geez. I should have known better than to hire an ex-government agent if I wanted to keep my past in the past."

"Wade wouldn't betray you," Tara said, her eyes bright with annoyance.

How long had it been since somebody defended him instead of the other way around? Even playing college ball, he'd protected the quarterback. "I'm not interested in your past," he said to his boss, shortly before shifting his attention back to the remarkable woman at his side. "I wanted Tara to know it's not her fault she didn't get the wedding contract."

She brushed her lips across his cheek. "Thank you."

She smelled like vanilla *and* chocolate. How much was a man supposed to endure for the sake of his job? Bullets he could handle, but not sweet devotion and chocolate-scented breath. This party certainly couldn't end fast enough.

"If you two need a moment alone..." Maynard began, again attempting to escape his stool.

Wade held him in place. "We do, in fact, but for your benefit, sir, I'd like to add that it's never a good idea to make a deal with a blackmailer. They always come back wanting more. Now, if you don't mind, I'd like to ask the DJ to play something slow. I'm going to take a ten-minute break to dance with Tara."

Wade wrapped his hand around Tara's and took a single step when Maynard said, "Wait."

Maybe the old guy isn't as tough as he thinks. "Sir?" Wade asked, turning toward him.

"I cheated on my wife," he said, his tone low, and he looked around to be sure he wasn't overheard. "Not the current one. The first one. Junior's mother."

Tara covered his hand with hers. "And Carla's P.I. found out?"

"Yeah." His face flushed with embarrassment, he sipped his whiskey. "It was a onetime thing. With a stripper, for pity's sake. I confessed to my ex, but she couldn't get past it. We divorced, and she promised never to tell our son if I'd swear I'd change. Neither of us wanted our boy growing up with a lecher for a father. And I did change—sorta anyway. I've had a lot of wives and lovers, but no mistresses. I never strayed again."

At least as long as divorce and prenups were available in bulk, Wade thought. But he admired his employer for wanting to protect his kid.

Maynard gripped his glass like a lifeline. "Junior can't find out his old man is a cheater when he's about to marry the girl of his dreams."

That witch Carla had impeccable timing. And absolutely no

conscience. Handy when you had a catering business and couldn't cook or manage your staff worth a crap. "I'd imagine Carla not only forced you to hire her, but threatened to go to the gossip magazines, too."

Maynard jerked his head in a nod.

"She's absolutely awful," Tara said, patting his hand.

"I'll help you get rid of her," Wade said, crossing his arms over his chest.

Hope lit Maynard's eyes. "How?"

"We'll talk about it when we get back to Austin." Wade was fairly certain he could get the P.I.'s bookies to call in some markers. And somebody from vice at the Austin P.D. would probably be interested in Posh Events' little side business. "Enjoy your weekend. Even if the food is lousy." He cast a glance at Tara, who nodded. "And I bet we can find somebody who has a good relationship with the resort staff to improve the meal for tomorrow night's reception."

Maynard jumped to his feet, and this time Wade let him. He pumped both of their hands. "I'll pay. I'll pay well."

Tara kissed his cheek. "Seems to me you already have."

A ridiculous spurt of possession darted through Wade's veins. "But we're still billing you."

"Sure, sure." Maynard shook their hands again, then strolled off with a definite spring in his step.

Wade found himself smiling as he watched the glittering crowd embrace his boss on the dance floor. "Fighting the bad guys is pretty damn cool."

Tara laid her hands on either side of his face. "You shouldn't have interfered. Though I'm obviously glad you did."

"You needed me."

"I did, but how did you know the right moment to show up?"

He leaned down, anticipating the moment her lips would merge with his. "Just one of those little superhero gifts."

8

Tara sighed as a warm hand slid slowly over her hip.

When the fingers of that hand dipped between her legs, the sigh became a moan.

The aroused male embracing her from behind brushed his lips across her shoulder. Though she knew she wasn't dreaming, she didn't open her eyes but lifted her arms to hook them around Wade's neck.

The hand not currently making her breathless glided up her torso, cupping her breast. She arched her back, pressing her body farther into his heated touch. His erection swelled, and she recalled the pleasure they'd shared during the night.

Unfortunately, duty called today.

It was no doubt early morning, as Wade had told her his ritual waking time was 6:00 a.m.

But for now only the two of them mattered. The world with all its complications and uncertainties waited beyond the door. Shut out.

Her breath hitched as desire tumbled into pure need. Turning in his arms, she covered his mouth with hers. Their tongues tangled. He clutched her against his bare body.

She gloried in the erotic sensations jumping through her. She wanted and ached. Wrapped around him as surely as a blanket, she wondered how they could ever be separated.

But the world would call, so she had to grab this glimmer of pleasure while she could. When the weekend was over, she wasn't sure what they'd have. She wanted something more and thought he might, too, but they'd shifted from strangers to lovers with dizzying speed.

Come Sunday, it could all be over.

Rolling, he moved to his back, still holding her tight. She straddled him, and he held up the condom packet between two fingers. She snatched it, knowing he liked her protecting him. The deed done, she loomed over him, kissing him long and deep before her hips inched their way over his erection.

"Do it again," he whispered against her throat.

She obliged, lifting herself to the tip of his penis, then pushing back down with infinite slowness. He closed his eyes and gripped her hips.

After a single night in his arms, she knew he was gathering his strength, fighting to hold back and draw out the pleasure for both of them. She rocked slowly, then increased the speed and pressure when the itch became too great not to satisfy.

She hit the peak a heartbeat before he did, her body convulsing around him, drawing him deeper inside, binding him…at least for the moment.

As she collapsed onto his chest, she inhaled the scent of his skin, reveled in the warmth of his touch—and she longed for more, for them to have a chance at finding out if there was more.

Yesterday they'd agreed to dinner when they got back to Austin, but she imagined there were a great many temporary women in Wade's past. His job defined him, probably always would. Was he capable of commitment? Was she?

Her job was her passion, her life.

Yet they'd struggled at their professions, each betrayed by circumstances they had no way to control. Was this thing between them a reaction, a solution or a beginning?

"I have to go," he said quietly, his hand gliding across her back.

"I know."

Still, neither one of them budged.

"You could come to spa day," he suggested. "Maynard owes you a princess-style treatment."

"He doesn't. He was protecting his family."

"He still screwed you."

Grinning, she lifted her head.

Wade's eyes sparkled with silver as he rolled them. "Okay, maybe he doesn't have exactly that pleasure."

"That one's elusive. Reserved for the best." She pressed her lips to his. "I'm the one who owes you a massage."

He rolled them again, then swung her into the cradle of his arms. "And I intend to collect very soon."

She was a pretty self-sufficient woman, but she liked being held so securely, so confidently.

Wade Cooper was a *man*. A broad-shouldered, commitment-oriented, honor-bound man that, frankly, she thought the world could use a lot more of.

He'd set her down beside the shower when a phone rang. "That's mine," he said, then kissed her forehead. "Don't get too soapy without me."

She turned on the water as she heard him answer the phone. Stepping under the hot spray, she closed her eyes. Without the burden of spying and confronting J. D. Maynard Sr., she could actually relax and enjoy the beach if she wanted.

When she got home, she had hope for the success of her business. Though she still wasn't sure how she'd counteract Carla's underhanded tactics, she finally understood the problem and was confident she'd find a solution. There had to be something illegal about using a catering business as a front for extortion.

"I have to go."

Tara rubbed the water from her eyes and opened them. Wade was peeking around the curtain. His hungry gaze roamed her body before settling on her face. "Now?"

"Unfortunately. And you need to come, too."

"Me?"

"Maynard Sr. was on the phone. The caterer's gone AWOL."

"COME ON," WADE SAID, holding hands with Tara. "Paul spotted her."

For the past hour, they'd been searching every corner of the resort for Carla and her staff, who weren't adhering to the schedule and bringing chocolate-covered strawberries to the bridal party, who were at the spa, or prepping the reception dinner. Since the resort staff had specifically set aside a work area for Posh Events in their kitchen, they were annoyed. The groom's father was worried. Wade was pissed. The bridal party, thankfully immersed in oxygen facials and seaweed wraps, were oblivious.

"Where?" Tara asked Wade as they strode through the hotel lobby.

"Calling a cab from the valet stand."

"What?"

"With her luggage."

"Why?"

"Don't know, but I've got a pretty good guess."

Her mind whirling, Tara searched for reasons and could come up with only one. A really bad one. "She can't be bailing out. The wedding is in less than twelve hours."

"Something's got her running. Maynard's behind this, I'll bet."

"You think he actually fired her? But that would mean…"

"That would mean he finally manned-up and took responsibility for his mistake." Wade maneuvered them around a young couple on their way to the door. "Bad timing, though."

"I'll say."

Though Tara didn't know Junior or Holly, she felt horrible that their luxurious island wedding might end in disaster. Every bride and groom deserved to feel special on their big day. They couldn't leave the glowing ceremony and not have the party of their dreams.

The one that had, in fact, already been paid for.

But surely Carla and her staff had begun setting up the reception ballroom and the beach tents last night. The preparations for a wedding this elaborate took many long hours. And Carla couldn't be leaving. A big fish like Maynard Sr. wasn't something she'd let get away—even if she was a ruthless, unethical bitch.

As the automatic doors between the hotel lobby and the front drive swooshed open, Tara nearly stumbled.

Carla stood outside, arguing with the valet, her designer luggage scattered around her.

How could she abandon her clients? Didn't she have *any* integrity?

"Going somewhere, Ms. Castalano?" Wade asked as he approached her.

"What—" She whirled, then glared at Wade. "Oh, it's you. And you," she added, focusing on Tara. "How did you get here? You're not invited."

"I'm a personal friend of the groom's father," Tara shot back.

"In your dreams, honey." Carla smirked. "Not that I care. I'm off to the airport. I've had enough of this tacky affair."

"So Maynard did fire you," Wade said.

"I quit."

"You signed a contract," Wade reminded her.

"After the way I've been treated, I'm certain my lawyer will fix that. I can't be expected to work under these abysmal conditions."

Wade tracked his gaze around their luxurious surroundings. "Yeah. Tough gig."

"I've had absolutely no cooperation from the idiot staff here, and my client had the nerve to complain about my performance." Carla examined her manicure—which looked fresh—as if that were the most important task on her agenda. "Of course I reminded him I've got three tabloids on speed dial."

She was ruining the wedding *and* spilling Maynard's secret? "What are the bride and groom supposed to do about the reception this late?" Tara asked in disbelief.

Carla's smile was malicious. "As of 2:00 a.m. this morning, that's no longer my problem."

Tara fought back a frustrated groan. What the devil had Maynard done? Couldn't he have waited until after the wedding to give Carla a piece of his mind?

Wade's eyes flashed dangerously. He lowered his voice and leaned close to Carla. "You might have the press on the line, however, you might want to remember that certain people you employ have weaknesses of their own."

Carla looked as if she'd swallowed one of her own horrible canapés.

"Loan sharks are such nasty characters," Wade continued. "I'd hate to see what they might do to that shiny new downtown office of yours."

"How do you—" Carla snapped her jaw closed so quickly it was a wonder her teeth didn't shatter. She recovered quickly, though. "Is that Cooper with a *C* or a *K?*"

"*C.*"

Carla punched keys on her cell phone, no doubt entering information about Wade. "I'm sure a pathetic rent-a-cop like yourself has a skeleton or two he'd rather stay in the closet."

Wade looked amused. "I certainly have some secrets. But then the Treasury Department is fairly protective of their own."

As Carla's confidence changed to confusion, a cab pulled in front of the hotel, and the valets jumped to store Carla's luggage in the trunk. No doubt, they'd be as glad to get rid of her as everybody else.

Wade opened the back door. "Have a nice trip, Ms. Castalano. I have the feeling we'll be talking again real soon."

"Sure we will." With one last flip of her hair, she was inside the car and gone.

Tara dusted her hands together. "Good riddance."

The valets, their gazes following the cab as it rolled away, grinned.

"Feel like catering a high-profile wedding reception?" Wade asked her.

"I'd already planned to help." She smiled confidentially, though she grew dizzy as she considered all the work to be done. "Are there really two reception locations and two concerts during the receptions?"

"Yep."

She linked arms with him. "I hope you brought your cape, your power ring and the entire superhero posse."

9

"PAUL, YOU MIGHT NOT KNOW a fake ID from a hole in the ground, but you do have a way with icicle lights."

Glancing past Tara to Wade, Paul flushed, but Wade didn't think the compliment was completely unwelcome. When they all got back home to Austin, he figured mutual business cooperation might go hand in hand with more hot romance.

One thing was certain—he had no intention of leaving his relationship with Tara on the island. They might have jumped into this whole thing pretty damn fast, but he was going to make sure they slowed down for a little savoring once they closed the book on the weekend.

"Well?" Tara asked this all-important question as she turned a circle in the middle of the ballroom where one half of Junior and Holly's reception was due to start in just under two hours.

Wade clasped her hand in his, giving it a supportive squeeze. "Perfect."

And he didn't just mean the decorations.

After consulting with the resort's head chef, giving the kitchen team some recipes and letting them add their own specialties, Tara, Paul and the banquet staff had begun to tackle the immense task of turning the blank canvas of the ballroom, plus the beach behind the hotel into the sleek island fantasy the bride had requested for the ceremony and reception. Well, technically, reception*s*.

The ceremony was to take place on the beach under tents, along with the buffet, surrounded by a centerpiece fountain of a dolphin and sea horses, no less. Outdoors was the country concert, featuring singer Mack Street. Inside was a pop concert, with a dance floor and light show.

Tara had called a wedding planner she knew back in Texas, who'd helped her design a backdrop with blue, purple and pink gossamer material purchased from the dress shop's alterations department. Long buffet tables had been draped in white linen. The resort florist had used some of the basic flowers already ordered, but had been thrilled to be given free rein in adding her own touch of tropical glamour.

They'd made the most of what they had, as well as adding a few inspirations when lacking. The valets were seen swiping palms and other greenery from various parts of the hotel and bringing them to the ballroom. Tara had convinced the manager to dig into the holiday decorations to supplement the twinkling ambience.

And Wade's security crew helped hang and place it all.

It was a team effort. Something Carla could never hope to understand or appreciate.

Wade had spent the day calming down the groom, the bride, the groom's father, then alternating among the three.

From Secret Service agent to gun-toting babysitter. Yet, strangely, he wasn't discouraged by the transition.

He was part of a winning team again.

Tara leaned against him. "Let's hope Junior and Holly like it, because I have to go cook now."

Wade braced his hands on either side of her face. "My beautiful warrior."

Her eyebrows winged up. "Yours, huh?"

He kissed her—long enough and thoroughly enough to

have the workers in the ballroom hooting and whistling. "Oh, yeah."

She held on to him, the regret to part clear in her blue eyes. "I do have a staff who can cook."

"I have a staff who's decorating."

"So I guess you need to go."

"Uh-huh." But he still didn't loosen his hold on her.

"How's the wedding party?" Tara asked, laying her head against his chest as if she planned to spend the rest of the day there.

"Getting ready in their suites, though the groomsmen have called room service twice already for more rum, so who knows whether the guys will actually make it to the ceremony."

"Is the press behaving?"

"So far. But then they're both awed by and afraid of me."

She giggled and leaned back. "Spotted any more crashers?"

"Nope. Besides, I caught the only one who matters."

She searched his gaze. There was more to say, but no time to do it now. "Maybe we could find some time to talk later?"

He pressed his lips against hers one last time. "Among other things."

As he turned to go back to his duties, Tara shouted, "Hey, Paul! You know anything about rolling out fondant?"

As pop singer Simone Leah moved into the pink spotlight and launched into her latest pulse-pounding hit, Tara took her first sip of champagne.

The bride and groom, plus their family and friends, had been dazzled by the decor. The seafood buffet was a hit. The signature cocktail of soda water, tropical juices and local rum had been indulged in by many.

Some a little too much. But what was a celebrity wedding except over-the-top indulgence?

Still, drama and last-minute scrambling aside, the loving couple had pledged their lives to each other beside the crashing ocean waves and in front of everybody who mattered to them. They were thrilled, and a happy client made for a happy caterer.

"It's a damn fine party, Tara."

Turning, she smiled at J. D. Maynard Sr. "Thanks, sir."

"I don't know how you pulled it off, but I'm grateful. My business, as well as anybody's within shouting distance of me, is yours."

"I appreciate the offer, and believe me, I'll take you up on it." Her gaze moved to Junior and Holly, holding each other on the dance floor. "But business isn't the only thing in my life anymore."

"Wade's a fine man."

Unfortunately Wade had his hands full with tipsy guests and rogue photographers attempting to pose as waiters, so she couldn't tell him that herself for quite a while.

"Just because something starts impulsively doesn't mean it can't work out long-term."

Tara angled her head. "This is an odd conversation to be having with you."

"Yeah, well, after all my marriages, I've figured out some things."

"Like the value of a solid prenup?"

J.D. paused as he was about to take a sip of his whiskey. "You're a sassy young lady."

"Sure, but—"

J.D. wrapped his arm around her waist. "I like sassy. Wanna be wife number five?"

"Ah…no." One randy Texan was about all she could handle at a time. "Thanks all the same."

"You're gonna need to take your hands off her immediately, Mr. Maynard."

Speaking of which…

Tara extricated herself from J.D.'s arms and moved to Wade's side. "J.D. was just congratulating us on a job well done."

Wade stared at his boss. "He can do that with his mouth, not his hands."

Tara expelled a lustful sigh. She was a self-assured, independent woman and all, but that possessive streak was sexy as hell. "He was. I thought you were tied up keeping out the press."

"Did that. Tossed 'em in the ocean."

J.D. coughed. Tara laughed and wrapped her arms around Wade's waist. "That's probably not a good idea. You'll only be compelled to go save them later."

He studied her. "Will I?"

"Yeah. You know, superhero code and all that."

His eyes silver with desire, Wade slid his thumb across her cheek, and Tara wondered how quickly they could fade into the background of the party. With all the bonuses J.D. had offered to the hotel staff to make sure everything went off flawlessly, they had a full cleanup crew ready to go.

J.D. raised his glass to them. "Make sure I'm invited to your wedding."

Shaking her head, Tara watched him walk away. "That man has a serious nuptials addiction."

"Maybe, but he's right. I love you."

Tara's head lurched around toward Wade. "You what?"

"I love you."

Even though the same thought had crossed Tara's mind, she didn't see how she could be in love. They hadn't had time for feelings to get that deep. "But— Are you serious?"

"Never been more so."

He sure looked serious. Her heart pounded, reminding her of her own commitment to make a relationship with him work. Was she being ridiculously impulsive or had she found way more than just her confidence the past few days?

"J.D. seems to think we can move beyond this weekend," she said slowly.

"I'm not sure that's encouraging."

"Good point." She searched his gaze for doubt and found none. "You and me? It's crazy. We don't even know each other."

He shrugged those amazing, strong, broad shoulders. "So we'll learn."

Impulsively she threw her arms around his neck. He lifted her so her feet dangled off the floor. "I love you, too."

His arms contracted around her. He kissed her temple and exhaled a breath that felt like relief. "I was hoping."

They were both taking a big chance on an island romance that had begun with them as adversaries who had only failing careers as the focus in their lives. But the risks weren't scary. And the rewards exponential.

"Let's get out of here," he said, setting her on her feet and guiding her from the glittering ballroom. "I planned a private party for the rest of the night."

"For us?"

"Guest list of two. Plus a chocolate fountain."

Her steps faltered, but he kept them moving. "I *really* love you."

"I figured that would do it."

* * * * *

SECRET ENCOUNTER

Jillian Burns

This story is dedicated to
hard-working teachers everywhere.

Acknowledgments:

This story came about due to the wonderful idea
of the hidden Mayan Codices plot given to me
by my dearest friend and
Rita® Award-winning author, Evelyn Vaughn.
College English teacher by day,
and my best TV buddy by night;
I couldn't have done this one without you, Von.

1

WHY ON EARTH HAD SHE thought she could do this?

Peyton Monahan squinted out the window of her taxi at the exclusive Rapture Island Resort, but the whole scene was a blur. She switched the designer sunglasses she wore for her prescription glasses and then wished she hadn't.

Lush palms and vibrant pink hibiscus headlined the expertly landscaped entrance to the hotel, beckoning her inside, but the armed guards in dark uniforms with headsets and clipboards? She shrank into the seat. Maybe she should fly straight back to Princeton and forget this crazy idea.

"Este es el hotel, la señora," the cab driver said. "Are you sure you don't want me to bring you to the front door?"

"No, gracias, señor." Peyton paid him and got out around the corner from the entrance. She couldn't be seen getting out of a taxi.

After the cabbie drove off, she stood there hugging a Gucci bag to her chest and bit her lip. Her entire professional career was riding on this. If she didn't get into this wedding, her dreams of locating the Mayan codices would go up in smoke.

Stick to the plan, Monahan.

Step One: Use her disguise to get past security.

Step Two: Find Mr. Edward Prescott.

Step Three: Convince him to fund the Mayan expedition to Mexico to find the codices.

Hopefully, she'd be in and out of the hotel before anyone was the wiser.

Focused on the guards, she crossed the lawn to the circular drive.

A cherry-red sports car roared past her and screeched to a halt at the valet's podium. A sandy-haired Greek god jumped out wearing a bright Hawaiian shirt and khaki cargo shorts that revealed long, muscular legs. He reached into the passenger seat for a black leather garment bag. As he bent over, Peyton couldn't help but admire his taut gluteus maximus.

The man glanced at her, sweeping his eyes up and down her body as he slung his bag over one broad shoulder. Her stomach tightened, and Peyton spun away, pretending to stare at the sky. Could she be any more lame?

From the corner of her eye, she watched him stride to the valet and hand him his keys, no doubt warning him about scratching the precious car.

Oh, the trials and tribulations of the rich and famous. *Get used to it, Monahan.* This place was going to be swarming with them. *And she was disguised as the belle of the ball.* Gathering her courage, she yanked off her thick glasses, replaced them with the sunglasses and approached the front doors.

A stone-faced security guard glanced at her, and then did a double take. "Ms. Addison?" His brows drew together.

Breath short and hands shaking, Peyton channeled her I'm-a-star-and-you're-not attitude, strode up the steps and brushed past the guard with a small smile and a wave.

The guard gave her a confused nod, then his gaze darted behind her. "Invitation, sir?" he asked, dismissing Peyton.

That was it? She'd done it! Suz had been right. Her assistant had sworn that with the right blond wig, some makeup and designer clothes Peyton could pass for *the* Holly Addison: movie star and celebrity bride of the "wedding of the century."

Striding through the revolving doors, Peyton glanced over her shoulder to see the man from the red car pulling a cream envelope from his shorts pocket. If only lowly language professors received invitations to celebrity weddings. Then she wouldn't have been reduced to this.

Peyton stopped in the glass-ceilinged lobby and let out a shaky breath. Now all she had to do was find a restroom, remove the wig and then she could hunt for Mr. Prescott unnoticed.

Squinting to see her surroundings clearly, she dug her glasses from her bag and slipped them on, and the world came back into focus. She scanned the area in several directions. Surely there was a ladies' room close by. Her gaze stopped at the escalator leading from the second level.

Holly Addison—the real Holly Addison—was headed straight for her!

The movie star hadn't seen her yet, but Peyton's mind blanked. *Come on, Monahan, think!* She hadn't flown this far just to get thrown out now. Should she yank off the wig and brave Holly and her entourage? But she had her hair pinned up inside an old stocking. Or should she turn her back and hope she wouldn't get noticed? With this long, silver-blond hair? What could she hide behind? The potted palms? Too short and thin.

The man from the red car sauntered past, headed toward the registration desk. Before she had time to consider the consequences, she threw her arms around the guy's neck. "Darling! I've been waiting for you."

The man stiffened beneath her arms.

She heard Holly speaking as she approached. "I don't care. It's my wedding and everyone should wear whatever I want them to."

The gorgeous guy glanced at Holly, and Peyton maneuvered him around until his large frame hid her from view. The longest second of her life ensued waiting to see if he would shove her away and call security.

But instead, he slid his arms around her waist and flashed a wicked grin. "Sweetie! Sorry I was late." He swooped down and covered her mouth with his.

Wide-eyed, she almost pulled away, but his lips moved over hers so softly, so sensually. Her body was melting and she opened her lips to him and—then his were gone.

Incredulous, she stared up at him.

One sandy brow rose as if challenging her to complain. His soft musky cologne filled her nostrils and sent an image of sweaty nights on cool sheets straight to her brain. And affected other parts she'd feared had amnesia. But no, they were alive and... remembering very well.

The Greek god in her arms watched the now-disappearing Holly and her entourage, and then returned his attention to Peyton. "That was fun, but now you need to convince me not to call security." Without warning, he pulled her wig off. The stocking and pins came off with it and her dark brown hair tumbled down in a tangled mess.

"Hey!" Peyton scowled and reached for the wig, but he moved it behind his back. She folded her arms across her chest. "So I wear a Holly Addison wig. That's not against the law."

"No, but stalking is. Tell me I didn't just help some psycho fan crash this wedding."

She clicked her tongue with disgust. "Of course it's nothing like that. I—I'm—I was hired to impersonate Holly as part of the entertainment for tonight."

He moved close. "Then why were you hiding from the real Holly Addison?"

"I—I'm supposed to be a surprise."

A corner of his mouth quirked up and his gaze had lowered to her lips and then to her. Under his intense scrutiny her nipples tightened and her breathing hitched. Wow. That had happened with a man exactly *never* in her life. She looked up into golden-brown eyes filled with the knowledge of her body's reaction to him.

"Why don't you convince me over drinks?"

"Drinks?"

His lips curved in a slow smile. "That's the going rate for my silence."

He wanted to have drinks with her? Guess Suz had been right about men being easily attracted by cleavage. Unfortunately, Peyton had missed Feminine Wiles 101 by spending her formative years in her boarding school's library.

"Look. I assure you I have no violent intentions against anyone, so feel free to enjoy the festivities with a clear conscience."

"Smile." He pulled out his cell phone and snapped her photo, and then he crossed his arms and waited.

He had her picture now, and he seemed to have no compunctions about calling a guard to have her thrown out if she couldn't convince him she was harmless. She smiled and tried batting her lashes. "I guess one drink wouldn't hurt."

"Good." His beautiful white teeth flashed in a smile so stunning, Peyton could only stare. "I'm Quinn Smith, by the way." He extended his hand, offering her back the wig.

Quinn. The name suited him. His face was a study in anthropological perfection, with a Roman nose and strong chin. And he was just unshaven enough to make his sensual lips stand out. His dark blond hair was cut short yet tousled enough to give it a just-ran-his-hands-through-it look.

But Mr. Smith was at this wedding because he was either a celebrity friend of Holly Addison's or a very rich friend of the groom, J. D. Maynard, heir to the wealthiest oil and ranch tycoon in Texas. Smith might as well have Spoiled Playboy stamped on his forehead.

"And you are?"

She realized she'd never taken the wig and grabbed it. She'd been too busy gawking at the man. "Peyton M-Miller." Inwardly, she cringed. *Really, Monahan? A false last name?* It's not as if she had a criminal record.

"All right, Peyton Miller." He checked an expensive-looking watch on his left wrist. "They're serving a buffet dinner on the terrace at six." He scooped up his garment bag where it had fallen and hitched the strap over his shoulder. "Meet me there in an hour."

The terrace. An hour. Smiling her promise, she nodded.

Smith narrowed his eyes at her, and then sauntered off to the registration desk.

She let out a relieved breath. With any luck, in an hour she'd be back in a taxi on her way to the airport. Now, to carry out part two of her plan: find Mr. Edward Prescott. Unfortunately, she had no idea what he looked like. Stuffing the wig into her tote, she pulled out the only picture she had of him, found when she'd looked up Prescott Industries on Google. The Google image was at least a decade old.

Owner and CEO of one of the United States' largest manufacturing conglomerates, Edward Q. Prescott was a New Jersey magnate, and an alumnus and patron of Princeton. He'd funded past excavations back when her father had run the Archaeology Department, but the last few years Prescott had become a recluse. No one in academic circles had seen him or been able to contact him.

Then, her department chair had heard through the university grapevine that Prescott would be attending the Maynard/Addison wedding. Thank the stars for gossipy secretaries. It seemed the groom's father, Maynard Sr., was a powerful enough business associate to force Prescott out of seclusion.

It was only a rumor, but Peyton was desperate enough to take the chance. All the other possible patrons had been hit by the economic downturn, and the Mexican government had offers from several other universities. If she couldn't come up with the financial backing soon, she'd lose her bid to locate the hidden codices. And possibly her career along with it.

Where to start? This hotel was larger than some small towns. There were a half dozen restaurants, a casino, three pools and an entire level dedicated to shopping. After scanning the lobby in the vain hope the CEO would suddenly materialize, Peyton grabbed her cell phone from the tote, dialed the hotel's registration desk and asked for Mr. Prescott's room.

"One moment, please," the woman said.

Peyton closed her eyes. *Come on. Be there.*

"I'm sorry, no Mr. Prescott has checked in."

"Thank you." Peyton closed her phone. She'd already sent the man three letters and called his office dozens of times. All without any reply. But he was the only one who hadn't given her a definite no. She only wanted a chance to make her case in person.

She made her way to a set of sofas with a view of the hotel's entrance, and waited. He had to show up soon. Didn't he?

QUINN RODE THE ELEVATOR up to the correct floor and stepped into his room as if on autopilot. He couldn't get the brazen brunette out of his mind.

There'd been a time in his life when risking arrest had come as naturally as breathing. It had taken facing five-to-ten in the state pen to convince him he might want to explore other options. But there still lurked a part of him that needed the rush of breaking the rules and damn the consequences.

And, it seemed, he'd found a kindred spirit.

He had a lot of questions for Peyton Miller. Like, what would she have done if he'd called security?

Maybe he shouldn't have trusted that she would meet him in an hour, but he'd learned a thing or two about judging the opposition while running Prescott Industries, and Peyton had been way too determined to crash this shindig. No way she'd leave without getting what she came for. Which was probably to scoop a story for her gossip rag.

But she hadn't tried to hit him up for any dirt on the bride or groom.

In any case, he intended to discover her secret. He hadn't been this intrigued by a woman in years.

Not that his schedule left him much time for women, intriguing or otherwise. But this weekend should remedy that.

He strode to the balcony doors and pushed them open. A warm breeze blew in and he drew in a deep breath of salty air. The steady crash of waves against the shore relaxed his shoulders. This is what he'd needed. How long had it been since he'd taken time off? Hell, even most weekends were spent at the office. Nine years he'd worked for the old man, and he could count his vacation days on one hand.

When Edward had received the invitation to the Maynard/ Addison wedding on Rapture Island, Quinn had jumped at the chance to get away. He figured he was a Prescott in all but name, and Maynard was an important business contact. No way the old man would go, not in his condition. And Prescott Industries needed to be represented at an event of this magnitude.

He'd had his assistant clear his calendar and begun fantasizing about a carefree weekend with a long-legged, suntanned woman. Three whole days to party hard, to make up for almost a decade of sixteen-hour days and watching Edward deteriorate from a ruthless tyrant to a paralyzed stroke victim.

Quinn preferred the tyrant. As much as the old man had made Quinn's life hell for years, Quinn hated to see that steel-trap mind stuck inside a failing body.

But he didn't want to think about Edward right now. He wanted to spend the weekend soaking up the sun, and getting laid. And not necessarily in that order.

His BlackBerry vibrated, but he ignored it and started to unpack, stashing condoms in the bedside drawer. Wait. The hotel had Wi-Fi. Wouldn't hurt to do a search on Peyton Miller.

He pulled his BlackBerry out of his pocket, replied to his assistant's text about the Jenson file and then got online. But none of the Peyton Millers he found on Google were reporters or even had a blog about celebrities. He was more intrigued than ever. As soon as he'd showered and changed into something slightly more formal for dinner, he made his way to the terrace.

The aroma of grilled steaks and salmon wafting in from an outdoor kitchen made his mouth water. And the sight of the curvy wedding crasher waiting for him at the French doors made his pulse race. She was still wearing the same short dress and green shoes from earlier, but her large bag was missing.

Her long brunette hair had been tamed somewhat, but it still curled deliciously around her shoulders. And her thick eyeglasses gave her a studious look that had him fantasizing about seducing a stern librarian.

As he reached her side, he extended his elbow. "Shall we get a table? I'm starving."

She frowned and ignored his arm. "All right."

Was that…annoyance on her face? That sort of reaction could hurt a lesser guy's ego. Amused, he pushed through the crowd and spoke to the maître'd, who led them to a small wrought iron table. White lights twinkled in the trees above them and employees were lighting torches placed at intervals along the stone path that led down to the beach.

After they sat, she crossed her legs and then uncrossed them, yanked on her skirt and crossed them again.

Quinn watched her, unable to keep from chuckling. "You good now?"

She straightened her shoulders. "Yes."

Their waiter appeared, and Quinn ordered a glass of dark lager, and then turned to her. "What will you have?"

She cleared her throat and twisted a paper napkin into shreds. "How many ounces of rum are in your frozen piña colada?"

Once the waiter informed her, she ordered the drink, but she had to have extra pineapple—on the side.

Fascinating.

They each ordered something from the grill, and then Quinn sat back to study the intriguing woman as she fidgeted with the sugar packets on the table.

Her eyes were the same bottle-green as in the pattern of her dress. But as he watched, they changed shades to more of a hazel as the rays of the sun caught her face.

Once their drinks arrived, Peyton pounced on hers as if she'd been lost in the Sahara for a decade. Her lips wrapped around the straw and Quinn's attention was drawn to her mouth. They were exotic lips, plump and expressive. He had to look away as he sipped his lager. Man, his social life had gone through too long a dry spell if that's all it took for him to be ready.

"So. There are eighteen Peyton Millers in the United States."

She choked on her drink. "You looked me up?"

"Ten of whom are men."

Her eyes widened. "Really?"

"There's a Peyton Miller in Houston, but I don't detect a Texas twang in your speech like the Maynards'."

"I'm not from Houston." She gave him a tight smile.

Superb deflection. Only confirming information he already knew. He could use someone like her on his mergers and acquisitions team.

Their food arrived and he cut into his steak, forked the bite into his mouth and chewed. "There was a Peyton Miller in L.A. But you can't be a friend of Holly's, or you wouldn't have avoided her earlier." He watched her closely as she pushed the salmon around on her plate.

"I also called every celebrity impersonator business and none of them have a Holly look-alike."

She hesitated for a fraction of a second. "Well, maybe I freelance." She took a satisfied bite of fish.

Another nonanswer.

"So, how about you, Mr. Smith?"

"Quinn."

"Quinn. Friend of the bride or groom?"

"Groom. His father and mine are business associates."

"Oh, and what does your father do?" She sipped more of her drink and then bit into the pineapple wedge. Juice dripped down her chin and she blotted it with her napkin.

Two things Quinn refused to discuss this weekend: his job, and his father. "I came here to get away from work and relax. So, for the next three days, company talk is strictly forbidden."

She raised her brows. "You work?"

Ouch. He grabbed his chest and mimed pulling out a dagger. "You really know how to hurt a guy's ego."

At least she had the grace to look sheepish. "Sorry." She lowered her gaze and slurped the last of her piña colada through the straw. "Mmm, that was delicious."

"Want another?" He raised a hand to motion to the waiter.

"Oh. No."

"No?" He dropped his arm.

"If I were to consume two piña coladas the rum-to-body-weight ratio would bring my blood alcohol level over the legal limit."

Quinn blinked. "But you're not driving anywhere tonight, are you?" Had she gotten a room here for the night? The only luggage he'd seen was that bag.

She grimaced. "Unfortunately, I had no choice but to get a room. However, my objective is to remain clearheaded."

Clearheaded? That was the last thing he wanted to be the next few days. "Why?"

She frowned. "Why what?"

"Well, I don't know about you, but I'm on vacation. And my objective is to cut loose and have fun." He pushed his plate away. "Let's walk on the beach."

She frowned. "Uh…"

"We're on a tropical island. When in Rome…"

"Oh, I'd almost forgotten." Excitement sparked in her eyes and her face became animated. "Tonight's a new moon and the next couple of nights you should be able to see a rare meteor shower." She scooted back her chair and stood before he could assist her out of her seat. "Maybe one more drink wouldn't hurt."

Quinn couldn't help but grin. They stopped at the bar on the way and she ordered another frilly umbrella drink. As she sipped it, he gestured for her to precede him down the path and then placed a guiding palm on the small of her back. Her curvy hips and perfect backside swayed in front of him as he followed. She was no anorexic starlet. Her figure was generous in all the right places, and that dress showed it off just as it should. And she was tall. He liked that he didn't have to bend his six-foot-two frame to kiss her.

And he *was* going to kiss her again.

2

THE WARM PRESSURE OF Quinn's hand on her spine made Peyton shiver. He'd changed into a forest-green dress shirt, charcoal slacks and a dark sport coat that enhanced his broad chest and shoulders, the sleeves tight over biceps that definitely got a workout.

Once they came to the end of the stone path, she bent a leg behind her and removed one high heel, then the other.

"Allow me." He took the shoes from her and they walked down to the shoreline. They turned left and strolled along the coast in a companionable silence. The sand felt heavenly between her toes, and the white foam from the waves glowed iridescent. The warm, salty air wrapped itself around her like a comforting blanket. Maybe Quinn was right. She might as well make use of her surroundings to reduce stress while she was here.

Her search for Mr. Prescott had been a failure this afternoon. Even paying for one night at this place would mean digging into her savings.

But how lucky that this wedding had put her so close to the equator at this particular date in time. She looked up and scanned the sky until she found the Summer Triangle, then pointed out toward the sea. "You see those stars just above the eastern horizon that form a triangle?"

He stepped close and his gaze followed her index finger. "Yes."

"In June, the three brightest stars are Altair in the constellation of Aquila, Vega in the constellation of Lyra, and Deneb, the brightest star in Cygnus, the swan." She pointed to each of them as she spoke.

"I never noticed that." He turned his head and she could feel his eyes on her. He was so near his nose brushed her cheek.

Drawing in a shaky breath, she continued, "If we had a telescope you'd be able to see Cygnus's long tail stretching along the Milky Way."

"I'll ask the staff to get us one." His warm breath tickled along the skin at her temple.

The stars went out of focus, and she had to concentrate to clear her vision. "What time is it?"

He checked his watch. "A little after seven."

"Oh." He wasn't touching her anywhere, but she felt his presence beside her like a giant jaguar poised to pounce on its prey.

"Why?"

"You won't be able to view the meteor shower until around 2:00 a.m."

"I thought meteors didn't show up until August."

"Oh, these aren't the Perseids. These are the Aurigids and they're extremely rare. They've been seen only a few times throughout history. The last time was 1911. And before that, the year 82 B.C." She turned to face him. He was staring at her lips. "So." She swallowed. "You…could see a comet that came by during the rein of—" he lowered his head and her gaze fell to his mouth "—Julius Caesar." Her final words came out a whisper as his lips closed in on hers.

What was he doing? She wasn't here for romance. She pulled back and located the constellations once more. Why was this gorgeous man focusing his attention on her? He could have any woman in this hotel.

Peyton's former boyfriend Jason had given more consideration to his arachnids than to her. But then, to be fair, she'd spent the past six months completely wrapped up in translating the Spanish monk's diary. Jason had run a distant third to sleep. No wonder he'd moved out. Well, that and the fact that he'd been sexting with an assistant in the molecular biology department.

Her throat was dry. She remembered her drink, took out the straw and gulped down the concoction.

"You might want to slow down or you'll get a brain freeze."

"What?" She glanced at the blond god standing beside her and a sharp pain burst in her frontal lobe. "Ooowww." She gripped her temples. Her eyes watered and she squeezed them shut.

"Here, try this." He slid one hand beneath her hair at the back of her neck and massaged her nape. At the same time he placed his palm over her forehead and gently pressed.

The pain slowly subsided and all she could feel were his hands on her skin, radiating heat, melting her bones and making her body tingle with awareness.

Her eyes still closed, she moaned and every muscle relaxed.

"Better now?" His warm breath tickled her ear as he moved her hair behind her shoulder and touched his lips to her neck.

"Yes," she said, her voice breathy.

The hand on her forehead slid down to cup her cheek. His thumb caught under her chin and tilted her head as he kissed his way down to her shoulder. Thought ceased. Her world shrank to the sensation of his firm lips burning a path along her neck.

"Your skin is so soft," he murmured and nuzzled behind her ear.

Peyton might have moaned again; she wasn't sure.

"And you smell like…what is that scent?" He inhaled deeply and then nibbled her lobe.

"Uh, it's just something I picked up." She had no idea what perfume her sister had sprayed on her this morning. All she could smell was his cologne. It steamed around her from the heat generating between them and the aroma started her veins pulsing. "Quinn." Her breathing was quivery.

"Hmm?" He nibbled his way along her jaw and over to her mouth. He paused, his lips a millimeter away from hers, and their gazes met. His light brown eyes conveyed his need.

And then she was kissing him, digging her fingers into his scalp, catching them in his dark blond hair. "This is crazy," she mumbled against his lips.

"It doesn't feel crazy," he answered, and deepened the kiss, angling his head. He caught her shoulders and pulled her against him. "Does it?"

Without breaking the kiss she shook her head. "Uh-uh."

His hand slid down to her waist and then crept up her rib cage, resting just under her breast.

On a gasp she pulled back. "I don't even know you."

"I'd like you to know me." He took her hand and pulled her toward the hotel, and she followed. *Am I really going to do this? Go to bed with a virtual stranger?*

Before they stepped into the brighter lights of the terrace, he caught her in his arms, cupped her face and kissed her hard and quick. Yes. She was.

As he led her across the lobby, rational thought returned and she tried to analyze her situation logically. Mr. Prescott was obviously not arriving tonight as she'd been informed. Her department chair's assistant must have heard it wrong from Prescott's administrative assistant.

And it made sense. This was Thursday and the wedding wasn't until Saturday. Why would he fly down this early? He might not even arrive tomorrow.

Until then, perhaps she should get a good night's sleep.

Once at the elevator, he kissed her again, his mouth opening over hers, his tongue sweeping in as if to claim her.

Then again, she'd had many a good night's sleep. They were highly overrated.

Before she could process her reaction he'd backed her against the wall inside the elevator and pushed a knee between her legs. A sharp ache right there where his knee nudged her clit. The ache shot straight through her and promptly her knees weakened.

The next chance she had to think straight, she was headed down the hallway to his room. As Quinn dug his key card from his jacket pocket and inserted it in the door, Peyton gave up on common sense. How many opportunities would a nerdy languages professor get in her lifetime for hot, anonymous sex with a Hollywood hunk? This kind of chemistry happened rarely in life. For her? Probably never again.

Then Quinn had the door open and he wrapped his arms around her waist, lifted her into his room and kissed her while he kicked the door shut. Once his lips were on hers again, all thought completely dissolved.

His hands slid around from her waist and gripped her bottom, pressing her against a sizable erection. Her heart seemed to skip a beat.

She broke off the kiss. "Quinn?"

"Yeah?" He was breathing fast. His lips wet in the moonlight that shone in from the balcony. But his grip on her backside loosened and his hands fell to his sides. She knew if she said she'd changed her mind, he might be angry, but he'd let her go. He might be just the man to try something she'd only ever read about.

"Have you ever heard of Tantric sex?"

QUINN DIDN'T THINK IT was possible to be any more turned on than he already was. But something about a woman wearing such thick-lensed glasses uttering the words *Tantric sex* made him have to count to five and think about accounting ledgers.

He needed to get out more.

"Uh, Tantric as in Kama-Sutra-type stuff?"

"Basically. There's a lot more to Kama Sutra than sexual positions, especially when read in its original Sanskrit, but for the purposes of tonight?" She reached her arms around his neck and kissed him just under his jaw. "I've always wanted to see if what I read was true."

What was it about this woman? He'd been captivated from the first moment. And now she wanted to talk kinky sex positions? He was all in.

He angled his chin to give her mouth easy access to his neck. "I'm game, sweetheart."

Her hands slid under his jacket, pushed it off his shoulders and down his arms. He let it drop to the floor.

"Wait a minute. Did you just say you read it in the original Sanskrit?"

"Shh." She covered his lips with a finger. Then unbuttoned his shirt, untucked it from his slacks and placed her palms on his chest. "The first element of Tantric sex is breathing." She kissed down his throat to his collarbone. "Take a deep breath in. Slowly," she corrected as he inhaled.

"I'm your willing pupil." He looked down at her and finger-combed her hair behind her ears so he could see her face.

"Just breathe in slowly and exhale even slower." Her hands moved down below his rib cage to his diaphragm, and as he exhaled, she pushed in with her thumbs. This pushed more air from his lungs. "Hold that. Don't try to breathe in yet. Feel how your body is deprived of oxygen. It needs it to live." Her voice mesmerized him.

Just when he thought he couldn't *not* breathe in, she said, "Breathe in now, slowly." She moved her hands down to his belt and unbuckled and unzipped him. He stepped out of his slacks as she pushed him backward to sit on the small sofa.

Being undressed by a woman was damned erotic.

Quinn watched, fascinated, as she calmly reached behind to unzip her dress, tossing it onto the club chair.

He swallowed. This might kill him before she was done. Her bra and panties were sheer black lace and he could see her large nipples beneath the lace.

"Once you've mastered your breathing, the ritual kiss is placed on each of the body's energy points. First the forehead." She straddled his lap and brought her lips to his forehead. "Then the eyes." She lightly kissed both his eyes. "The cheeks." She matched deed to words. "The throat, the breasts." When her mouth settled over his nipple, his dick strained inside his briefs.

"The lips." She kissed his lips and licked them. "And the interior of the mouth." Her tongue swept inside to lap like a cat licking cream.

"Peyton." He gripped her waist to keep from pushing her down to the cushion and covering her body with his.

"Patience." She moved down between his legs and kissed his navel and the inside of his thighs. She moved back up and kissed each of his arms, then looked at him. Her eyes smoldered into his. "This may be followed by acts of the mouth on the *yonis* of the woman."

"I thought you'd never ask." He cupped her butt with both hands, and with her legs wrapped around his waist, carried her to the bedroom and laid her down on the bed.

She fell back and raised her arms above her head.

Quinn stood there a moment taking in the sight of her. Her hips and thighs were curvy, and her breasts were large. With trembling fingers he stripped her panties off, then sank to one knee beside the bed, grabbed her under her butt and pulled her toward his eager mouth.

At his first lick she cried out and jerked her hips. He smiled and dug in with his tongue, suckling at her clit. The more he played with her, the more she moaned and squirmed. Her chest rose and fell as her breathing became ragged. He brought his fingers up to part her and used a thumb to rub her clit. She stiffened and called his name along with a few words in some language that sounded like French.

Grabbing a packet from the drawer, he shoved his briefs off, and moved her farther onto the middle of the mattress. She reached behind her back and unhooked her bra, throwing it on the floor. Then almost as an afterthought, she took off her glasses and rolled to lay them on the bedside table behind her.

Ahh, her breasts were beautiful. He wanted to hold them, give them the attention they deserved. And he would. But right now he just needed to be inside her. He rolled on protection and entered her in one long thrust.

She gasped and he almost came right then. She was so tight and hot he had to hold still a second.

"Quinn." She moaned his name and he had to move. Determined to last until he'd made her come again, he pulled out and pushed back in, savoring the sensation of being inside a woman. There was nothing else like it. And he vowed not to go so long without this again.

His weight on one elbow, he cupped her breast and thumbed the tight nipple, watching it crinkle into a tiny bead.

She put her hand over his and encouraged him to squeeze and play with the breast. Her other hand massaged his shoulder, and then her fingers combed through the hair at his nape. Her nails dug in when he took her nipple in his mouth and tightened his lips around it.

Still moving in her, he switched to her other breast, worshipped its soft fullness and drew the nipple into his mouth.

"Quinn, faster."

She gasped when he complied and shifted his hips to change the angle of his thrusts.

Their gazes met and he allowed a sense of smugness into his smile when her eyes widened and she made a funny little sound.

"The lady approves?"

She squeezed her eyes shut and gave a quick little nod, then her face flushed pink and she stiffened beneath him. Oh, yeah. He let go and came with her, burying his nose in her neck and gritting his teeth as his orgasm hit him with the force of a tidal wave. He could feel his pulse pounding in his temples and even with his eyes closed the world seemed to spin.

When he could finally breathe again, he realized he'd collapsed and his full weight was on her. But when he tried to lift himself off, she tightened her arms around his back. She was breathing heavily, and her breasts rubbed against his chest. He'd never want a skinny woman again after having Peyton's cushiony flesh beneath him.

But he worried about squashing her so he wrapped his arms around her and rolled to his side, taking her with him.

"You okay?"

She let out a long sigh, her breath tickling his chest. "Who needs Kama Sutra when one has Quinn Smith?"

Quinn felt his head swell to twice its normal size. He knew his grin was cocky as he tightened his hold around her. "Aw, shucks, ma'am. Tweren't nuthin'."

She chuckled, a low, throaty sound. "Somehow I can't picture you with a cowboy hat like J. D. Maynard's."

"No?"

She shook her head, rubbing her forehead against his chest. The head shaking turned into nuzzling her cheek against his chest, then moving down to kiss and lick his nipples. Her hand strayed to his hip and moved around to cup his butt. She reared back her head and looked him in the eye. "Despite my thorough satisfaction moments ago, there are several other positions I'd like to try."

Her words riveted him, searing images into his brain he'd happily put into practice. He cleared his throat. "It may be a few minutes before I can accommodate you, but I'll give it my best."

She smiled at him and pulled his head close for a deep, long kiss.

Mmm, a naked woman in his arms, her skin touching his from breast to ankle. He could die happy right here. He broke the kiss and nuzzled down her neck. "I'll clean up and be right back."

"Okay." She nibbled on his ear. "And when you return, I'll tell you about something else I read and always wanted to experiment with."

"I'm just a big lab rat to you, huh?" He kissed down her throat to her collarbone.

She frowned. "Oh, no. I didn't mean it that way at all. It's just that I—"

"Hey." He raised his head and smoothed the worry line between her brows. "I was just kidding. It's fine. In fact, I love it."

"Oh." Her lips curved in an endearing little smile as she rolled her eyes. "I'm not always good with humor."

Their gazes met and something clicked inside him. He didn't have anything recent to compare it to, but it almost felt like…a connection. And tenderness. *Come on, Quinn. One good lay and all of a sudden she's your soul mate?* He heaved an exaggerated sigh and rolled to his back. "Being your guinea pig will be a supreme sacrifice, but someone's got to do it."

She giggled and rolled to face him. "Quinn?"

He tucked an arm beneath his head and glanced at her. "Yeah?"

She ran a finger around his chest, twirling it back and forth and around his nipples. "How would you like to have multiple orgasms and last all night?"

3

"HOUSEKEEPING," A HOTEL MAID called out as she knocked on Quinn's door.

Quinn jerked awake and winced as his muscles mutinied. What the hell?

Oh, yeah. He was on Rapture Island and he'd just had the most amazing sex in his freakin' life.

He opened his eyes. Sunlight filtered through the sheer curtains over the French doors of the balcony. He was naked, spread out in the middle of the mattress, lying on his stomach with his head hanging over the foot of the bed.

And Peyton was gone.

The things that woman had taught him. The muscle he'd learned to contract. He must have come a half dozen times before the big finale.

The maid knocked again. *"Señor?"*

He forced himself to lift his head and call out for her to come back later. It took a long hot shower and three cups of in-room coffee before he felt capable of coherent thought. Never in his life could he have imagined a night like that.

And then to wake up alone? For all he knew she could've left the hotel.

That thought shouldn't bother him. Perfect weekend fling, right? Except it bugged the hell out of him. What was her deal?

If she was still in the hotel, he intended to find out.

He stepped into shorts and pulled on a T-shirt, then headed down to the breakfast buffet, sore in places he didn't even know he could be sore.

He spied her sitting at a patio table outside the coffee shop. Fresh-faced, with her hair pulled back in a simple ponytail, she looked younger, more vulnerable. Her clothes were simple, too. Jeans and an orange-and-black Princeton University T-shirt. The sophisticated celebrity from yesterday was gone completely. Interesting. This persona fit her better. But she had a lot of explaining to do.

"You're taking this playing-hard-to-get game way too seriously," he said in a low voice as he slipped into the chair beside hers.

Choking on her coffee, she looked up from her newspaper, wide-eyed. Then she just blinked.

"You have nothing to say?"

"I'm not playing hard to get."

"No, but you're not who you say you are."

Her eyes got even wider. "Why do you think that?"

Quinn smiled. "I think after last night, I deserve the truth."

"What has last night got to do with anything?" There was an edge to her voice.

"Come on, Peyton. If I thought you were a stalker or a terrorist I would've turned you in already. I just want to know what's really going on."

"My name is Peyton Monahan. And I swear I've never done anything like this before."

"So, why?"

She took a sip of her coffee. "Perhaps I should start at the beginning."

He leaned back and folded his hands over his stomach, straightened his legs and crossed his ankles. "I'm all ears."

"Do you remember the horrible earthquake in Mexico City last year?"

Quinn nodded, completely enthralled. How the heck was she going to get from earthquake to wedding crasher?

"Well, they were digging through the rubble of this old church and found a diary written by this Spanish monk...but it was written in Mayan." She leaned forward and her eyes sparked with excitement. "You know how many people can read and translate ancient Mayan hieroglyphs?"

Before he could shrug, she continued, "Five. Only five people in the whole world. And I'm one of them."

Her lips turned up in a conspiratorial smile, and he could practically feel the waves of exhilaration.

"I couldn't believe I actually got to hold this book, much less got asked to translate it."

"Okay, you're, like, one of those museum curator types? Wait a minute. Is this going to turn into some *Da Vinci Code* mystery?"

She waved a hand, shook her head. "I'm a professor at Princeton. My doctorate is in archival science, but my specialty is ancient languages."

Quinn whistled, impressed. He'd barely managed to earn a simple business degree.

"Anyway, it turns out the diary is over four hundred years old."

"Whoa."

"I know, right? I wondered the same thing—what's a seventeenth-century Spanish monk doing writing his diary in Mayan? I mean, the diary was written when the Spanish were *burning* all the Mayan writings."

"Uh, yeah," Quinn nodded. "That's exactly what I was going to ask." Not.

She got this adorable little crinkle between her brows and she tilted her head. Then her expression cleared and the thrill returned to her eyes. "In his diary the monk claimed to have saved some of these writings from being burned. He wrote that he fled Tayasal and hid the codices in a cave. And I think I know where!"

She reached out and grabbed his hand and leaned even closer. "Do you know how rare these codices would be if we can find them? We've just got to retrieve them and secure their safe restoration." She squeezed his hand.

Quinn liked the feel of her hand in his. "You look almost as excited right now as you did in my bed last night."

Her smile dropped and she yanked her hand back. "What happens on Rapture Island stays on Rapture Island."

"Of course. But we're not back in the states yet."

She seemed to think about that a moment. "True."

"Look, all this Mayan history is interesting, but what's it got to d—"

"To do with this wedding? I need funding. I've tried everyone, but the recent economic problems have hit my usual patrons hard. My father suggested I ask a businessman who used to fund his expeditions years ago."

"Ahh, of course. And the rich dude is at this wedding? Who's the su— Uh...financier you're looking for?"

"His name is Edward Prescott. Ever heard of him?"

Quinn froze. Peyton kept talking, but he wasn't listening.

"—CEO of Prescott Industries."

Damn it.

"—ignored my letters. I heard he'd booked a flight to come here, and my father assured me he wouldn't miss attending this wedding."

Nothing like a little irony first thing in the morning. He wanted to laugh out loud.

"If I could just get five minutes alone with him, I know I could convince him to— Quinn? Are you okay?"

She was looking *for him.*

Since he'd been in charge of the company the past few years, he'd been the one to decide where Prescott Industries made their charitable contributions.

Bits and pieces of memories from work all came together to fit like a puzzle. *She* was that professor, the crazy old coot—or so he'd thought—that kept pestering his office the past couple of months requesting money for some antiquities expedition. And he'd pitched the letters in the trash and had his assistant block the phone calls.

"Quinn?"

He blinked and Peyton came back into focus. "Yeah. Just too much caffeine on an empty stomach." For the first time in his life he was glad his name was Smith and not Prescott. As a boy, he'd longed to be legitimate, a real Prescott. He'd have given anything for his father to acknowledge him as his son.

Damn. Something fun and exciting had just become complicated. Why did this woman have to come with an agenda?

Wait a minute. Did she already know who he was and hoped that sleeping with him would soften him up for the sales pitch?

He studied her face. She'd have to be one hell of an actress.

He could tell her who he was and see what she did next. Would she plead her case and then leave, having gotten what she wanted? Maybe. But he didn't want to take that chance. He'd had to practically beg her to tell him why she was here. Surely that meant she didn't know who he was. Besides, he wanted to spend more time with her. Without any problems getting in the way.

An idea was niggling its way into his brain. He vowed to tell her who he was tomorrow and take her request for funding under consideration as soon as he got back to the office. She'd had the chutzpah to crash this wedding—it seemed the least he could do. "So, this Prescott guy was supposed to arrive yesterday?"

"I thought I knew his schedule, but I figure he's got to show up eventually." She bit her lip. That gorgeous, plump lip that had done such amazing things to him last night.

Concentrate, Quinn. "I think I may have seen his yacht

docked in the bay yesterday." That was technically the truth. He'd decided to take a few extra days and sail his father's yacht down here from the Keys.

"You did? Oh, my gosh, I didn't even think of that. Of course. He must be such a recluse that he won't even stay in the hotel." Her expression shifted. Worry and distress creased her eyes. "But how can I approach him if he doesn't leave his yacht till the wedding?"

Guilt nudged him. He reached up and cupped her cheek. So soft. "He has to, at the very least, put in an appearance at the wedding tomorrow night. You can catch him then."

"But—"

He let his hand drop. "In the meantime, I booked an excursion extraordinaire for today. Come with me."

She shook her head. "I don't think—"

"Peyton." He sighed. "Paradise vacation? Fun? Remember?"

"Aren't there other people here you were planning on spending the day with?"

He shrugged. "The only people I know at this wedding are the Maynard's. I met Maynard Jr. and the newest Mrs. Maynard at a business luncheon one time. Mostly I deal with Maynard Sr."

"Oh." Her eyes, more blue than green this morning behind the glasses, blinked several times while Quinn held his breath waiting for her answer. Then she smiled. "I suppose it wouldn't make much sense to waste the airfare just to sit around in my room watching CNN."

PEYTON STEPPED INTO the body harness and pulled it up between her legs, while the instructor hooked her into the parachute. Her palms were sweaty and they trembled as she snapped on a life vest. She wasn't really going to do this, was she? She didn't do heights. She wasn't some crazy adrenaline junkie with something to prove.

"Ready?" the orchestrator of her demise asked, grinning like a wild man. The wind ruffled his hair, and Peyton didn't know what was more enticing—his smile or his strong hands snapping on his life vest as if he'd done this hundreds of times.

"Tell me again why I let you talk me into this?"

"You'll love it, I promise." Quinn's light brown eyes shone with mischief as he stepped into the double-body harness beside her.

He'd promised her a "thrilling experience" and she had to admit, looking out over the dazzling turquoise sea, with the white lines of breakers in the distance, the view from this grassy bluff was absolutely gorgeous. If only they could simply admire it from here while sitting on a nice soft blanket eating a picnic lunch.

But no, Mr. Insanity wanted to be pulled off a two-hundred-foot cliff at ninety miles an hour.

The instructor double-checked all the snaps and buckles, and the towrope, then gave the waiting motorboat a thumbs-up.

The crew returned the signal and the motorboat idled out. The instructor and his assistant held up both sides of the chute.

"Remember, resist the pull," Quinn urged. "Keep the line tight."

Their towline began to go taut until it was completely extended.

"Oh, god, I can't do this. Quinn, tell them to stop." She dug in her heels and gulped in too much air. She was going to hyperventilate.

"Peyton. Look at me."

His voice had taken on an edge she'd never heard before. It was a command, and she obeyed. His serious gaze captured hers. "I swear I won't let anything happen to you. You're safe. Do you believe me?"

Her breathing calmed and she nodded.

"Take my hand." He held out his hand and she latched on to it. "Good, now it's just three steps. You can do it." He squeezed her hand.

Peyton kept her eyes on Quinn as she stepped, one, two, three, and then there was nothing but air beneath her and she was flying over the Caribbean waters.

The wind tickled her bare feet and she finally returned Quinn's smile.

She looked out over the water. "Ohmigosh, Quinn!" She tapped his arm. "Look, dolphins." She pointed to their right, where she could just make out a pod of maybe a dozen or more gray fins breaking the surface and disappearing again.

"I'll see if I can get the boat to take us closer." He put action to words, gesturing for the water crew to head farther out to sea.

Once they were closer to the fast-traveling pod, Quinn nudged her arm and offered her a waterproof disposable camera.

Peyton snapped a few pictures and spent the next hour marveling at the beauty of the world around her.

A few smaller islands could be seen once they cleared the crescent-shaped bay of Rapture Island. Some were towering lone peaks, jutting out from the sea like otherworldly pillars.

Before she was ready, it was time to land. The motorboat slowed and she and Quinn gently drifted downward. As soon as they splashed into the water, Quinn reached behind them and unhooked them from the chute, and the boat swung around to pick them up.

Quinn climbed in first, and then extended his hand to her. She clasped it, his palm warm and his fingers strong as they wrapped around her and lifted her into the boat with ease. Heat surrounded her as she landed against him. He kept hold of her hand and used his other arm to slide around her waist and pull her close. She felt the tremor in his breathing and sympathized. She was finding it hard to take a deep breath herself.

"Thank you."

He frowned. "For what?"

"For encouraging me to do this. I'd never have had the guts to parasail. It was the most exhilarating thing I've ever done."

His teeth flashed in a grin. "I find that hard to believe." At the word *hard,* he moved his hips and his erection nudged her stomach. "Maybe we should forget the rest of the outings for today and go back to the room." He nuzzled her temple and nibbled her ear.

"What…" She was having a difficult time concentrating as his lips kissed down her neck. "What other outings?"

"Eles devem receber uma sala." The boat driver spoke in Portuguese to his assistant and they both snickered.

Mortified, Peyton pulled out of Quinn's hold, grabbed a towel and covered herself. Then she moved to the seat at the back of the boat.

Quinn narrowed his eyes, a ticked-off glint in them. Glancing at the boatmen, he took a towel and sat beside her. "Did they insult you?"

"No." She examined her nails and bit a cuticle. "The driver said we should get a room."

Quinn's grin returned. "Isn't that what I was saying?" His grin faded. "I thought after last night…"

"No, it's not that. I just don't like making a spectacle of myself in public. It's uncalled-for."

"That sounds like something my great-aunt Esther would say."

"It may sound old-fashioned, but causing a big scene never generates positive results."

"That bad, huh?"

"What?"

"Your childhood. Sounds like you were never allowed to be a kid."

Irrational anger bubbled up inside her. "My father did the best he could after my mother died."

"Hey, I'm sorry." He reached for her hand but she moved away. "How old were you?"

A ridiculous lump formed in her throat. "Two."

He whistled. "That's a long time, just you and your dad." He took her hand between his and she let him.

"My dad was busy. I—I went to boarding school."

He grimaced. "Sounds miserable."

Feeling the need to defend her dad, she shook her head. "Boarding school was great. I had access to a substantial research center and one of the best science curriculums in the country."

"But didn't you miss your dad?"

How had they gotten started on this personal subject? And why were all these uncomfortable emotions creeping up after all these years? "He…had important studies. He didn't need me bugging him."

"Bugging him? Growing up, I was pissed I didn't have a dad, but at least I knew my mom wanted me."

Peyton turned away, squeezed her eyes closed. It'd been her fault her father hadn't wanted her around. Her fault she'd been sent off to boarding school. *Pull it together, Monahan. Quinn doesn't want to deal with your messy emotions any more than your father did.*

But what had he said about his dad? Something wasn't right. Wait. She pulled her hand out from in between his. "I thought you said your dad was a colleague of Maynard's?"

Quinn blinked. "Uh…yeah. He decided he wanted to be a part of my life after his wife died. He didn't have any other kids."

The boat pulled up to the dock and the assistant hopped out to tie the rope. Quinn shook the driver's hand, and the driver wished them both a good day.

Peyton extended her hand. *"Obrigado pela maravilhosa experiência,"* she said, enjoying watching the boatman squirm when he realized she'd understood what he'd said.

Quinn took her hand and helped her step off the boat, then kept holding it as they headed back along the dock to the beach. "That wasn't Spanish, was it? How many languages do you speak?"

"No, it was Portuguese. And I speak seven fluently, but I can only read and write five. I'm learning Arabic now."

"Arabic." He frowned.

Darn it. Why'd she have to have such a big mouth? The guy

could probably care less about what language she was learning. And she'd babbled on about her childhood. If he had any doubts about her being a total nerd, she'd just dispelled them.

"What languages do you speak fluently?"

She looked up at him as they entered the hotel and let her hand slip from his. "That's a boring subject. Why don't you tell me about what you do?"

He looked away, his gaze following a couple headed down a causeway past a sign that read, Addison-Maynard Wedding Rehearsal and Dinner. "I told you, I refuse to think about business this weekend." His smile and the fact that he took her hand in his again softened his refusal. "Hungry?"

The change of subject caught her off guard. "Starved."

"Shall we try one of the restaurants?" He did no more than hold her hand and ask the unspoken with his eyes.

She returned his smile. "Let's order room service."

$$4$$

AFTER SHOWERING IN HER own room, Peyton dressed in the same T-shirt and jeans she'd worn briefly this morning, then stuffed a clean shirt and undies in her bag. Good thing she'd packed for the whole weekend just in case. And the dress she'd arrived in would do for the wedding.

She traveled up in the elevator and knocked on Quinn's door. He'd won the "which room" argument because his had a balcony.

Quinn opened the door and Peyton stopped short. A small table had been set in the suite's large living area with fresh flowers, a candle and gleaming silver dome-covered plates. Quinn moved to stand behind a chair with a look of anticipation.

He'd showered and shaved and as she neared she could smell his unique cologne, an intoxicating blend of sandalwood and… something dark and mysterious.

The scent didn't match the man she knew. Except, when she thought back to last night, she remembered how intensely he'd made love.

He pulled out the chair and gestured for her to sit. "M'lady?" The dark suit coat and slacks he wore told her he was accustomed to dressing for dinner, even when alone in a hotel room. And the pale lavender dress shirt fit him so well it had to have been tailor-made for him. No tie at least. His open collar emphasized the strong column of his throat. He looked tanned, healthy and way out of her league.

Wiping her hands on her worn jeans, she gingerly sat, resisting the urge to take off her glasses and pull her hair out of the ponytail. "I think I'm way underdressed."

"You're beautiful," he said as he took his seat opposite her.

Beautiful? Maybe this guy was as blind as she was without her glasses. She could rationalize his attraction last night with her hair and makeup all expertly applied by a professional and the designer clothes Suz had chosen to emphasize her less-than-thin figure. But tonight? The man must suppose a bird in the hand was worth two in the bush.

Ah, well, who was she to complain? One more fantastic night with a handsome, charming man who made love to her as though she was the only woman in the world? There'd be no objections from the peanut gallery.

"Let's eat." He uncovered plates of filet mignon, shrimp linguini and pizza.

That surprised a chuckle out of her. "Pizza?"

He shrugged, looking endearingly sheepish. "I wasn't sure what you liked."

Since when had anyone ever treated her like this? Like a queen. Her father had tried one Christmas. She'd been seven and her dad had taken her out to dinner. But she'd resented him spending so much time at work and begged him not to go back to the university after the meal. He'd told her not to be so melodramatic and had left her with the nanny.

If only she'd learned her lesson that night she might not have been sent off to boarding school.

Peyton studied the man across from her. He'd been so easygoing all day. But this wasn't real life. Eventually, messy emotions emerged and who wanted to deal with that?

"Peyton? Where'd you go?"

She shook her head and focused on the plates in front of her with a wide smile. "Sorry, just…a little overwhelmed."

"Well, how about a tiny bite of everything?" He served her a small portion from each entrée.

It all looked delicious, but Peyton couldn't taste a thing. As much as she tried to caution herself to resist Quinn's charms, she found herself laughing at his quick wit, drawn to his vibrant masculinity. Which was not smart. But once she talked to Prescott, she'd be gone, and she'd never see Quinn again, so what was one more night of fantasy?

After they'd finished the meal, he wiped his mouth on a napkin, then came around to pull out her chair. "And now for surprise number two." As she stood, he bent and kissed the back of her neck.

She shivered. "You're numbering them?" Just like last night, her voice had gone all breathy.

"Mmm." His lips kissed down to the neckline of her T-shirt. "Maybe I should make you wait for the second one."

"Maybe you shouldn't." She turned, cupped his face and used her tongue to slowly, sensually explore his mouth.

He scooped her up, carried her to the bed and laid her on the mattress, following her down and taking control of the kiss. Long, powerful, intense. She'd never been the focus of such concentrated passion.

"Peyton." He palmed her cheek, then ran his fingers into her hair and pulled out the band holding her ponytail.

Leaning on one elbow, he moved his hand down and slid it under her shirt to cup her satin-covered breast. A low rumble sounded from his throat as his mouth nuzzled between her breasts. He dragged the hem of her shirt up over her other breast to gain access to it.

Her nipples hardened to tight, aching peaks under his skilled mouth and tongue. "I think you have too many clothes on." She slid his suit coat off his shoulders and he helped her pull his arms out and toss the coat away. Then she palmed his erection and unzipped his slacks.

She tried to free him from his briefs, but when he pulled her T-shirt up over her head she had to raise her arms. He took advantage of her captured arms and unhooked her bra, dragging it and her glasses off along with her shirt. With a low groan he cupped her breasts in his large, warm hands and gently squeezed.

Not to be thwarted, she returned to her mission and clasped his hard length. She suddenly craved to do something she'd never thought she enjoyed. Maneuvering herself to lay with her head at his groin, she took just the tip of him into her mouth, teasing it with her tongue.

Quinn made a growling sound low in his throat and fumbled with the button on his slacks until he could shove his pants and underwear down and off. "I'll give you thirty hours to stop that."

Peyton smiled. "The Kama Sutra calls this *Nimitta*. Touching." Next, she clamped her lips over the shaft. "This is called *Parshvatoddashta*. Biting at the sides." She raised her head and stroked him several times, then pressed sucking kisses down the length. "*Chumbitaka*. Kissing."

As she flicked her tongue all over his penis and then tapped it repeatedly on the sensitive glans tip Quinn fell back, his arm covering his eyes. "Peyton. You're killing me."

"That is *Parimrshtaka*. Striking at the tip."

"No kidding," he choked out.

She glanced back. His chest rose and fell in harsh breaths. He still wore his shirt, and the sight of him naked from the waist down stirred something deep inside her. He looked sexy and vulnerable and completely masculine all at the same time.

Seized by a wild passion, she took him deep into her mouth, pulled on him and sucked hard. "*Amrachushita*. Sucking a mango." She took him deeper, enjoying the silky flesh moving over the rigid shaft, drawing him out slowly and pumping him with her hand.

He moaned and rose up. "Okay, that's enough." Cupping her face in his hands, he kissed her.

"But there's one last step," she protested. "I work upon your lingam with my lips and tongue until you spend. That is *Sangara*." She gave him an evil grin. "Swallowed whole."

His raised one brow. "That ain't gonna happen." He wrestled her jeans and underwear off, pushed her thighs apart and lowered his mouth to her clit.

She gasped and stilled, lost in the feel of his tongue licking her and delving deep. But she still had access to him. She took him deep, but couldn't do the job justice with the distraction he was creating between her legs. Her hips rolled unconsciously as he brought her ever closer to completion.

But just as she felt ready, he lifted his head.

She whimpered her disapproval.

"I want to be in you when you come."

She wanted that, too, and held out her arms.

He tugged off his shirt, grabbed a packet from the table and moved over her, fitting himself between her thighs. "Peyton." The way he said her name, so tenderly. There was wonder in his eyes as he ran the back of his hand down her cheek and then finger-combed her hair away from her eyes.

Her throat tightened trying to hold in emotions she'd never felt before. How could she have such strong feelings for someone she'd known barely twenty-four hours? Logic told her she couldn't. She was simply caught up in the moment.

He lowered his head and kissed her, entering her at the same time. The thrust of his tongue matched the rhythm he set with his hips and the dual sensation gave *eroticism* new meaning.

Within a few strokes she was again at the edge of that cliff. And like this afternoon when they went parasailing, when he whispered in her ear, "Come with me," she did. Her body tightened, her stomach dropped, the world around her reeled. She clung to his back as he thrust one last time and then stiffened above her, a vein in his temple straining.

As he hung his head beside hers and nosed into her neck, she ran a hand down his back and up again, tracing his long spine. His breathing still labored, he took her mouth in a kiss that felt different. It was gentle and filled with some unnamed emotion. The fingers of her other hand ran through his hair as her feelings swirled in confusion.

His lips left hers slowly and he glanced at her with a troubled look in his eyes before he rolled away and padded to the bathroom. After a few minutes in the shower, a tall, white blur emerged. Peyton reached for her glasses.

Quinn was wearing a thick, white robe and carried a matching one for her. "Now for surprise number two." He extended the robe to her.

"You mean that wasn't your surprise?" She nodded toward the bed with a suggestive smile as he helped her slip on the robe and tie the belt.

He wrapped his arms around her waist from behind and she felt his chin on the top of her head. "You didn't see that coming, huh?"

She giggled—giggled! —and turned in his arms. "Yeah, I guess I kind of did." She flattened her palms on his chest. "Surprise me, Smith."

He smiled down at her, took her hand and led her out to the balcony. Front and center stood a large telescope mounted on a tripod. She gasped and moved to look into the eyepiece, automatically finding a star and adjusting the lens for a clearer picture.

"I told you I'd get you one," he murmured into her ear.

Peyton's senses filled with the scent of Quinn, of warm sea air brushing her skin, of the sound of waves crashing to shore, of glittering stars in the black sky. Her chest constricted against the emotion welling up inside her. "Thank you."

He nodded and turned his attention to the stars. "Now we can really see that meteor shower." He glanced at his bare left wrist. "In about…three hours. What *will* we do to pass the time?" He grinned.

She giggled. Again. She never giggled. It was so...unprofessor-like. Something unruly children did. And then fathers sent them out of the room. Wow. Talk about an aha moment. Had she purposely kept herself from doing fun and silly things? Never allowing herself to laugh or enjoy anything too much? Or get angry, either. She didn't allow herself to feel anything too deeply. Including passion. But oh, this night was made for passion.

Turning in his arms, she clasped her hands around his neck. "I think we can find something to do." His lips had almost touched hers when she pulled back. "Do you play Scrabble?"

He frowned. "What?"

She smirked. "Gotcha." Her mouth found his.

He deepened the kiss, tightening his hold around her waist. She began untying his belt, but he stepped back. "I almost forgot."

Peyton barely stifled a whine of disappointment. "What?" He had to go somewhere?

"Surprise number three."

Ridiculous relief washed over her as he wiggled his brows and led her by the hand into the suite. Who was this needy woman in her body? It seemed that once she'd decided to stop checking her emotions at the security gate, all kinds of baggage was pouring out. "There's more?"

With a nod, Quinn disappeared into the bedroom and came back carrying a long plastic garment bag. It was from the hotel's clothing boutique.

"What'd you do?" After scrutinizing him a moment, she opened the bag and pulled out the most gorgeous dress Peyton had ever seen. It was a midnight-blue silk organza strapless gown with beading around an empire waist. Her mouth hung open.

"Do you like it? It's for the wedding tomorrow."

Her mind reeled. He'd bought her a dress? "Why did you do this?"

"You need something to wear."

"Well, I was just going to wear the dress I had on yesterday."

He was shaking his head before she finished speaking. "This is Holly Addison's wedding we're talking about. I overheard two women in the surf shop while you were trying on bathing suits. Holly is thinking of mandating that all guests must wear red, white or blue in honor of her groom's state flag."

"She has? Can she do that?"

He shrugged. "If you feel uncomfortable I'll have it returned."

"No, no. I just…" She searched the inside seams for a price tag. "I'd like to reimburse you." Even if it took her the other half of a year's salary.

"No way." He claimed the dress from her and draped it across the sofa, then grasped her upper arms. "I shouldn't have bought it. It was stupid and impulsive and—I just feel responsible for you having to attend this wedding."

"But why should you?"

He stared at her with a strange expression, as if she'd asked why the earth was round. But then he huffed a laugh and shook his head. "Forget it." He kissed her, deep and intense, his tongue playing with hers. He untied her robe and spent the next few hours making slow, purposeful love to her until she couldn't remember or care what they'd been discussing.

QUINN PUMPED HIS HIPS in one last hard thrust. Peyton's beautiful breasts bounced in his palms as she threw her head back and cried out. He closed his eyes and drew in a long, ragged breath as she collapsed on top of him.

Emotions overwhelmed him as he caressed her back, running his hands down to squeeze her fleshy butt. He was still hard inside her, could still feel tiny spasms of her orgasm as she straddled his hips.

"Mmm," she hummed, sounding well satisfied, and the purr reverberated against his chest where her cheek lay. Her hair tickled under his chin and her damp skin clung to his.

Suddenly he wanted to tell her who he really was. Guilt nicked him like a dull razor. He'd tricked her into staying today.

Unless she already knew who he was and was playing him for a sucker. If this was all some elaborate scheme… He swallowed a lump blocking his throat. He had to admit it would hurt, and not just his pride. Somehow this thing with Payton had grown into more than just a weekend of fantastic sex. He'd had great sex before, but this felt different.

Maybe he should get everything out in the open. Clear the air. No. First thing in the morning would be soon enough. He couldn't promise he'd write her department a check, but he'd give the expedition consideration. *If* she were being honest with him.

What would he be funding again? Searching for some Mayan diary a monk had hidden in a cave?

"Tell me about this monk you're looking for." At least he could go back to his shareholders with an explanation.

She raised her head and met his gaze. "It's not the monk I'm looking for, but rare Mayan codices that he saved from the Spanish's ethnic cleansing."

"So you're going spelunking?"

She grinned and rested her chin on top of her clasped hands. "Not me. I just interpreted the diary and could help locate the correct cave."

"How do you know which cave to look in?"

"I have a fairly good idea of the general vicinity based on his writings. His wife knew—"

"Wife? I thought he was a monk?"

"Oh." Her eyes sparked with excitement just as they had yesterday when she'd first told him about this. She crawled out of bed, retrieved her bag and dug out a plain brown book. "She's the reason the codices were saved at all. It's very romantic." She slid back into bed and Quinn pulled her close against him. He liked her skin touching his.

"This Spanish monk fell in love with a Mayan princess." She

opened the brown book to reveal small, precise handwriting. "Very Romeo and Juliet of them." She turned to a specific page. "Listen to this. 'My beloved sneaks past her guards and meets me at the fountain. Though it is dangerous if we are caught, I cannot regret our secret trysts. I would risk all for her love.'"

Peyton put the book down and drew a finger over his chest, playing with his nipple. He covered her hand, unable to concentrate with her doing that.

"Did it end tragically for them?"

"No. That's what's so cool about this story. They stole back as many of her people's scrolls as they could before the Spaniards started burning them. Then they ran off together. We know they made it to what is now Mexico City and lived a long and loving life together, but he was never able to go back for the writings. It just wasn't safe."

Quinn's alarm on his cell phone beeped. He reached for the phone and silenced it.

"What is it?" She sat up, leaning on one hand. With her hair falling wildly around her and the sheet draped over the lower half of her body, she could've been the inspiration behind some famous Grecian statue. Something in his chest contracted.

"Quinn?" Her brows creased. "Is everything okay?"

"You remind me of this statue I saw once in a picture of a fountain in Italy. Of a beautiful sea nymph."

Her eyes widened and she sat up, drew her knees to her chest and clasped her arms around them. "Only a picture? You've never been to Italy?" she asked quietly as she reached up to rub her eye.

"Not yet. You?"

"No, but I'd love to see it someday." She turned and smiled at him and he almost blurted out that he'd take her, that they'd go together. What was happening to him?

"So what was the alarm for?"

The meteor shower! He jumped out of bed and took her hand, pulling her with him. "Come on. The shower."

"Oh, my gosh, I can't believe I'd completely forgotten."

Grabbing their robes, he slipped one around her shoulders as they raced out to the balcony.

For the next thirty minutes Quinn witnessed the most amazing phenomenon of his life. The shooting stars fell across the black sky for so long and burned so brightly they seemed suspended in time. The telescope was forgotten as he drew Peyton against his chest and wrapped his arms around her waist.

It seemed the most natural thing in the world to hold her as he stared in awe at the heavens. Natural and right. He remembered what she said about Caesar witnessing these same meteors and felt humbled and insignificant. He exchanged glances with Peyton, and she looked at him as if he were the only man in the world she could've shared this with, as if he got her, and she got him and this connection was something special that he might not ever find with anyone else.

Damn. He knew in that moment he wasn't ready never to see her again after tomorrow. He wanted to know this woman better. To spend more time with her.

With a woman who didn't know who he really was.

5

PEYTON OPENED HER EYES slowly, feeling sluggish but oh-so comfortable and warm. She didn't want to get up.

Usually she awoke alert, already thinking about the day ahead and the work that needed doing. As she lay there, snuggled into a soft mattress, she knew there was something she had to accomplish today, but all she wanted to do was close her eyes and try to continue the dream she'd been having about a sexy man....

A heavy arm curved over her waist and a very masculine hand cupped her breast. Her eyes popped open.

Quinn was nestled behind her, spooning her. His finger and thumb rolled her nipple.

No. She must fight this urge to turn over and kiss him. She had a mission and it was time to get back to the real world. Her career depended on getting this funding. It was the only reason for being in this fantasyland to begin with.

She removed his hand and scooted out of the bed, racing for the bathroom without answering his mumbled protest.

Turning on the shower, she took a moment to examine herself in the mirror. She'd left her glasses on the bedside table and she wasn't going back for them. She brought her face a few inches away from the glass.

Her hair was mussed and tangled, her lips were red and swollen, and her cheeks and neck were chafed from his stubble.

My god. She looked…like a woman with a lover. Even when she'd first moved in with Jason she'd never looked like this in the morning. More importantly, she'd never felt so weak and jittery. As if she had a hangover, except she'd overindulged on emotions.

She stepped into the hot water and let it soak her hair. Could she replicate the job the makeup artist and hair stylist had done for the wedding? She didn't have all those products and appliances. She'd have to go to the salon here.

Closing her eyes under the spray, she tried to picture herself finding Mr. Prescott and what she would say to him when she did. But as she ran soap over her body, it seemed every part carried a memory of Quinn's hands or mouth caressing it.

Quinn.

Just thinking of his name caused her heart to flutter. Which was illogical. She'd known the man less than forty-eight hours. So he was a good—okay, she'd admit, an *amazing* lover—but that was most assuredly due to his making love to dozens, maybe hundreds of women.

These feelings were merely the result of getting caught up in the physical passion and in this fantastical situation. There was a reason she'd decided at an early age to never let emotions rule her. They confused and complicated everything. Calm, cool logic made life simple.

"Peyton?"

She jumped as Quinn stepped into the shower with her. He swung her around and kissed her as if he hadn't seen her in weeks.

"Good morning," he mumbled into her neck.

Mmm, all that gloriously naked, muscled man in her arms. Hers to run her hands over. His narrow hips. His taut butt. His shoulder blades and the muscles that bunched in his wide shoulders as he tightened his hold on her and deepened the kiss.

"Let's go back to bed and order room service," his deep voice rumbled behind her ear.

Oh, yes. That sounded wonderf— Wait a minute. She pulled out of his embrace. "I can't." But, oh, how she wanted to.

"Why not? The wedding isn't until six. And it's not even two."

"Two o'clock in the afternoon?" She grabbed the shampoo bottle, squirted a dollop into her palm, and began vigorously washing her hair. She never slept late.

"Here, let me help with that." Quinn ran his hands over her stomach and up her rib cage as if he worshipped every inch.

"Stop." She squirmed away from him.

He dropped his hands. "What's the matter?"

"Nothing, I just have a lot to do and think about." She turned her back to him and rinsed her hair. "I—I'm just not used to sharing my shower."

After a moment of silence, she turned to find he'd left the bathroom. Dressed in her jeans and shirt, she padded out to the living area. Quinn sat out on the balcony wearing shorts and a T-shirt, a baseball cap backward on his head. The morning sun glistened off the water and the golden hair of his tanned legs. He was having coffee and looked so ordinary, so cute, guilt wrenched in her chest.

She poured herself a cup of the coffee he'd made and joined him.

"Hey." She tried to smile.

His expression grim, he stared at her. "We need to talk."

"Isn't that usually the woman's line?" She gave a halfhearted laugh and avoided looking into his eyes.

He reached across the table and took her hand. "I need to tell you something."

Looking out over the turquoise water, she gulped her coffee. Was he going to tell her he was married? Or that it'd been fun, but he couldn't in good conscience let her crash the actual wedding? "You're going to call security on me if I go to the wedding, aren't you?"

"What? No. But…I haven't been completely honest."

Oh, no. "Then let's not do this." Snatching her hand away, she stood so fast her chair almost fell over. She didn't want to hear that he'd been lying. What good was a fantasy weekend fling if reality intruded? "Like you said yesterday, last night was what it was. You'll be going back to your life, and I'll go back to mine." That way, this interlude could always remain pure in her memories.

"No, this is important." His voice got louder. He stood, rounding the table to close the distance between them.

Her feet shuffled toward the French doors. "Can we talk later? I really need to get my hair and makeup done." Darting inside the suite, she gathered up her bag and headed for the bedroom. Whatever he had to say, she didn't want to hear it. Why did he have to complicate things with some deep, dark secret? It wasn't as if they would ever see each other again.

"Peyton." He followed her in from the balcony. "Wait."

Finding yesterday's clothes wadded up on the floor on the other side of the bed, she started stuffing them into her bag.

He came into the bedroom and grabbed her arm. "Will you stop and listen a minute?" he demanded.

Ah, there it was. So, he had a temper when he didn't get his way. He was just like she'd been as a little girl. This was what she'd avoided all her life. An emotional scene.

She faced his angry glare with detached calmness. "Let go of me, please."

His brows creased and his gaze lowered to where he gripped her arm. Jaw tight, he dropped his hand.

She brushed past him out of the bedroom to the main door, grabbed the latch and then glanced back. He stood in the bedroom doorway, his ball cap in his hand.

"Thank you for—" She swallowed. Damn it. Now it was ruined. A crushing wave of resentment and depression hit her hard. He'd spoiled everything. She pulled open the door and raced to the elevators.

WHAT THE HELL HAD just happened?

Quinn pitched his hat across the room. He ran a hand through his hair and paced to the kitchenette, turned and paced back to the bedroom doorway. Peyton's reaction made no sense. If she'd known all along who he was, wouldn't she have let him admit it and pretend ignorance? Or, if she didn't know, what was all that anger and evasion about?

He was sorely tempted to pack up, check out and forget about attending this wedding. He could sail the yacht back to Florida and maybe stop in the Bahamas along the way, take in some night life…. Damn it. He needed at least to put in an appearance at the reception. J. D. Maynard Sr. was too important a connection not to give the family his regards.

And what was he running from anyway? He'd tried to tell her the truth, albeit a little late. And he hadn't done anything she hadn't done. They'd both pretended to be someone else.

His mind made up to stay, he decided to hit the gym for a workout, swim some laps and then sit a spell in the sauna before dressing for the wedding. He pulled his tux from the closet and saw the garment bag with the dress in it. His chest felt tight. He wanted to kick himself for that colossal blunder.

Shoving it back in the closet, he turned and kicked something across the floor. The brown book. Peyton's translation of the monk's diary.

He picked it up and opened the page to the beginning.

AMAZING WHAT MAXING OUT a credit card could do for a girl.

For the second time in a week, Peyton had her hair and makeup done and a gown chosen by experts. The dress wasn't as beautiful as the one Quinn had bought for her, but the dark navy chiffon would do.

As she sat in the hairdresser's chair, it finally occurred to her that what Quinn had probably tried to tell her was that he'd lied about Prescott being on a yacht. The CEO had probably been in this hotel the whole time, and she'd wasted yesterday not look-ing for him.

She hadn't figured out why yet, but more than likely Quinn had been trying to shield his friend from the crazy professor out to get his money. Just thinking that's what Quinn thought of her made her cheeks hot with humiliation.

Hours later and, at last, within reach of her goal, she stood beside a stern-looking security guard waiting for Quinn. Her name wasn't on the guest list and she'd had to swallow her pride and tell him she was with Quinn Smith.

As she scanned the lobby watching for Quinn, he appeared from the elevator bank looking wickedly handsome in his black tuxedo. She tried not to stare but her eyes wouldn't obey her brain. He was staring at her, too, his gaze serious as he approached.

Without a word to her, he gave the security guard his name and vouched that Peyton was his plus one. Once outside, they walked under a trellis of gardenias, white roses and twinkling white lights. The air was fragranced with hundreds of brightly-colored tropical flowers.

Quinn placed his hand at her elbow and directed her to some folding chairs about halfway down the aisle. As if by agreement they waited in silence for the ceremony of the century.

Peyton scanned the hundreds of guests, searching for Prescott. Seeing no one that fit his description, panic gurgled in the pit of her stomach. She shouldn't have wasted yesterday with Quinn. Shouldn't have assumed Mr. Prescott would stay on his yacht the whole time. What if she'd missed him?

A string quartet began the wedding march and one by one seven bridesmaids came down the aisle. Then the bride appeared and everyone stood and faced her as she approached the altar.

Peyton glanced at the groom, who was waiting under the arch staring at his bride with all the love in his heart visible on his face.

What would it be like to be the recipient of such adoration? Peyton had always thought she didn't want marriage and kids, but watching Holly Addison, she envied the certainty in the bride's eyes. As the couple exchanged vows they'd written themselves, Peyton tried to suppress her emotions, but it was difficult not to get caught up in the fervor of the ceremony.

Not one but two receptions were being held. The younger crowd headed for the largest ballroom, where a pop diva was singing under flashing lights. It didn't seem like the kind of place Prescott would choose.

The other boasted a famous country singer who was married to an actress and friend of Holly's. Without asking Quinn, she followed the older crowd to a huge white tent on the resort grounds surrounded by palm trees and hibiscus and fountains with statuary of sea horses and dolphins. They reminded her of what Quinn had said about the sea nymphs in the Italian fountain.

She knew that fountain, the *Fontana dei Quattro Fiumi* in the city of Navona. When Quinn had mentioned it, the hairs on the back of her neck had risen. She'd always wanted to see that fountain of Neptune rising from the waves to rule over his sea creatures.

Good grief. *Snap out of it, Monahan,* Peyton admonished under her breath. With renewed determination, she searched the crowd for Mr. Prescott.

He wasn't at any of the round tables. He wasn't at either of the two bars or the cake table. Desperate, she casually asked a passing bridesmaid if she knew Mr. Prescott. No luck.

The band was setting up on a stage. A polished wood dance floor had been laid over the beach. Amid enthusiastic applause, the famous singer appeared at the mike and began a lively song about love being a leap of faith.

She felt Quinn's presence, quietly accompanying her as she moved around the room. A few inches taller than most of the men, he'd grabbed two glasses of champagne for them. His solid support tonight, despite her behavior earlier, humbled her.

Her hand trembled as she sipped her champagne. What if she'd made a huge mistake this afternoon? What if whatever he'd been going to tell her had nothing to do with Prescott, or being married, or about their weekend together at all?

But what else could he possibly want her to know?

As those thoughts seeped into her psyche, the groom led the bride out onto the dance floor. The tenor sang another hit about making memories.

It was a beautiful song. She watched the newlyweds dance, smiling and gazing into each other's eyes. Marriage definitely was a leap of faith. The odds of success were slim. The possibility of pain almost certain. Why did anyone risk it?

"Can we at least have one dance?" Quinn's deep voice murmured into her ear.

She turned to find his right hand extended, palm up.

Self-preservation battled with a powerful longing. She had to find Prescott, but all she wanted was to be in his arms one last time.

"It's just a dance, Peyton." Gently he took the champagne flute from her hand, set it on a tray and lightly grasped her hand. He led her out to the floor and slid his arm around her waist to rest at the small of her back.

He held her lightly, but close enough that her breasts pressed against his chest, his hip nestled into hers. Memories of the past two nights smothered her senses. As if in a dream, she placed her hand in his and followed him as he rocked from foot to foot and turned slowly around the floor.

His scent enveloped her and without thinking she laid her cheek against his chest. His hand moved around between her shoulder blades, bringing her closer. Her arm went over his shoulder and encircled his neck, and with her fingers she played in the hair at his nape.

Her other hand rested against his chest and she could've sworn she felt his heartbeat, strong and sure beneath her palm.

The song finished and the singer started another slow number.

As Quinn guided her around other couples in perfect rhythm to the steady beat, he caressed her back and his lips lightly touched her temple. As the music faded and came to an end, neither one of them moved. Gradually he let her go and stepped back. He led her off the dance floor to a shadowed corner where the setting sun and candlelight didn't quite reach.

He took both her hands in his and stared at them, rubbing his thumbs over her skin. "I just wanted to say—" he looked up and her gaze caught in his "—I'll never forget our time together, the meteor shower and...just you."

Her chest ached. She blinked away tears. It was crazy. She couldn't possibly feel so strongly for someone she'd just met. She didn't believe in love at first sight. But the words in the monk's diary mocked her pragmatic rationale. The Spaniard had spoken of losing his heart the very moment he first spied the young Mayan girl. And their love had lasted a lifetime....

"Mr. Smith?" A youngish blonde approached and laid her hand on Quinn's arm. "Quinn Smith, I'm so glad you came, darlin'." She spoke with a prominent Texas twang.

Quinn's face drained of emotion, except his eyes. They turned warily to the Texas lady. "Mrs. Maynard, how are you?"

This was Mrs. Maynard? She couldn't be much older than the groom.

"I couldn't be better, hon. But how's your daddy? We heard you'd been practically running Prescott Industries ever since his stroke."

It took a moment for the words to sink in. Peyton might not have even noticed except for Quinn's reaction. His gaze darted to her. His mouth dropped open, then shut again. Time froze as all the words jumbled around in her head and came back to her in bits and pieces. *Daddy. Running Prescott. Stroke.* Quinn's father was...Prescott?

She yanked her hand from Quinn's, spun on her heels and bolted through the crowd.

She was furious. Outraged. Mortified.

Quinn was Edward Prescott's son. He'd sat there and let her

run on and on about finding the man. He'd made up some bull about a yacht. How he must have been laughing behind her back.

And he'd slept with her! Knowing who she was. If she didn't find an exit soon she'd confront that SOB and cause a scene that would make her childhood tantrum pale in comparison. But Peyton Monahan didn't vomit her emotions into a room and leave everyone else to clean up the mess. Peyton Monahan removed herself from the situation.

Then she was running, jostling past guests and waiters. She searched frantically for an exit, finally spied the double doors, and then couldn't seem to reach them, no matter how fast she ran, it felt as if she were in a nightmare where everything was moving in slow motion.

Quinn's voice called to her from somewhere behind her, but she finally reached the doors, threw them open and raced through the lobby to the front drive and jumped into a cab.

She tried to say *airport,* but she couldn't get enough air in her lungs to speak. She was hyperventilating. A hand pounded on her window and she jumped and everything went back to real time.

"Peyton. I tried to tell you this morning." He looked down and reached for the door handle. She slammed her palm down on the lock at the same time. He looked back up at her, his mouth a tight line. "Peyton, unlock this door." He pounded on the window with the flat of his hand, and she flinched.

She called to the cab driver, "Airport. Now!"

The cab lurched out of the driveway and she watched Quinn from the back windshield as he stepped into the drive, staring after her.

6

WE'RE BACK IN KANSAS, TOTO.

Peyton didn't have a cute little dog, but as her plane landed at Newark in the wee hours of Sunday morning, she was definitely back in the real world. Though it was June, the air was chilly as she made her way out of the Jersey airport and hailed a cab. Colors seemed drab, less vibrant than in the Caribbean, and crowds of serious-minded people jostled past, intent on their own schedules.

Peyton felt right at home.

In the taxi, she pulled out her BlackBerry and checked her email and messages. Nothing that wouldn't wait until tomorrow, but it stunned her how she hadn't given her BlackBerry a thought the past three days. How could she have been so distracted from her life? Easy. Her distraction had been a candidate for Sexiest Man Alive, except he liked playing cruel games.

Now that she *was* back, it was time to think about alternative options for funding the Mayan expedition. If only she could get a loan and finance it herself. Even if she had anything to use as collateral there was no way she'd ever be able to repay the money. She'd just have to search farther afield for a benefactor.

By the time the cab pulled up in front of her apartment, exhaustion had hit. She trudged up to her third-floor unit feeling as if she weighed two tons. And as she sank into bed, her last vestiges of strength gave way to weak self-pity.

As plans go, this one had been a massive failure. What had she been thinking? Flying down to an exclusive resort? Crashing a celebrity wedding? All in the hopes of speaking to a man she didn't know and who had already shown he had no interest in her proposal.

Except, of course, the real man who'd been ignoring her letters and phone calls the past several months was Quinn Smith. He'd been "practically running" Prescott Industries since his father's stroke, so *he'd* known who she was the minute she divulged her real name.

Thinking back on her behavior that day in the lobby, she closed her eyes and cringed. Pretending to be Holly Addison was bad enough, but grabbing a complete stranger and kissing him? She hadn't fooled Quinn for one minute. And then to let him talk her into spending a whole day with him away from the resort. Of course, her quarry had been right under her nose the entire time.

She flipped onto her stomach, burying her face in her pillow. Could she be any more of an idiot?

IT TURNED OUT SHE COULD.

When she went to transfer the translated version of the diary from her travel bag to her briefcase Monday morning, it wasn't there. Panicked, she dumped the contents of the tote onto her bed and tossed every article across the room in a vain hope that the diary was hiding among her clothes and toiletries.

But it wasn't.

Peyton dropped to her knees by the bed and lowered her head into her hands. How could she have been so irresponsible?

The translation wasn't her only copy of course, but the idea of leaving it around for anyone to read was reprehensible. She'd have to call the airline company and the hotel to see if it turned up.

Trudging into the Anthropology building in a horrible funk,

she hadn't even made it to her office when her department chair called her and a few other faculty members to a meeting in the staff room.

"Congratulations, Dr. Monahan," Carolyn Whitehouse popped open a bottle of champagne as Peyton entered. Her colleagues' applause erupted around her, all of them smiling as if she'd just won the lottery.

Confused, Peyton watched glasses of champagne being passed around. "Dr. Whitehouse, what's this about?"

"The check arrived this morning by courier." Dr. Whitehouse lifted her drink. "To Dr. Monahan from Prescott Industries."

A cold chill shivered up Peyton's back. She dropped her smile. "What?"

"Now that we have the funding, I'd like you to begin assembling a team. Dr. Steinberg has asked to assist you and—"

"Wait," Peyton cut in. "Prescott Industries sent us a check?"

A stunned silence echoed around the room. "Peyton, we assumed *you* had secured this," Carolyn said. "I know you've been trying to meet with Mr. Prescott for months."

"Well, yes, but—"

"Don't be modest, Doctor. Prescott Industries came through." Dr. Whitehouse beamed as she held out the check.

Peyton took it, searching for the signature at the bottom. *Quinn Smith.*

She froze. The staggering amount would more than cover the expenses for the expedition. Fury spewed up from deep in her core. She barely restrained herself from ripping the check into shreds. *Keep it together, Monahan.* She did not do melodrama. She did not cause scenes.

After half listening to congratulations and Dr. Whitehouse's plans, Peyton locked herself in her office, staring at the check in her icy hands. Her vision had narrowed to a small tunnel of light and the image in front of her shook.

What could Quinn possibly think of her? To have it couriered over with no note or any explanation? Did he think he was paying her for services rendered? God!

In his defense, he had tried to tell her his identity. So he couldn't have thought she already knew.

Still, there were too many unanswered questions. Too much baggage attached with this check for her to accept it.

But how could she explain losing the funding now? The humiliating truth would come out, and Dr. Whitehouse would probably ask for her resignation.

How dare Quinn put her in this position.

She gathered her purse and stuffed the check inside, then stalked down the hall and out to the parking lot to her little car. Traffic seemed determined to thwart her. The normal twenty-minute drive to New Brunswick seemed to take twice as long. As she parked at Prescott Industries' corporate offices and entered the tastefully decorated lobby, she took several deep breaths to calm her temper.

"May I help you?" a security guard wearing a headset asked from behind a reception desk.

"Yes. I'm Professor Monahan and I'd like to speak with Quinn Smith, please."

"Just a moment." The guard punched some buttons on a phone and announced her name to whomever was on the other end.

Peyton's hands shook as she tried to smooth back loose strands of hair that had fallen from her chignon. *Remain calm, Monahan.* But she couldn't quite stop the churning in her stomach.

The guard's eyebrows rose as he hung up, studying Peyton curiously. "Sign in here, ma'am." The guard extended a clipboard with a sign-in sheet. "Then take the elevators to the eighth floor and turn left."

"Thank you."

On the eighth floor she was blocked once more by a woman at a desk. A gray-haired, no-nonsense woman. "I'm here to see Mr. Quinn Smith."

"Mr. Smith is in a meeting. If you'll have a seat he'll be with you in a moment."

Peyton eyed the door behind the administrative assistant. It sported an engraved gold plate that read Quinn Smith. *In a meeting, my Aston Martin!* A white haze of fury pumped adrenaline into her veins. The bold woman from Rapture Island who took chances and risked anything was on the loose. She pushed past the dragon lady and opened the door.

"Excuse me, you can't go in there!"

Quinn sat behind a large desk on the other end of a huge office. He pushed to his feet as she stomped up to the desk.

"I don't know who you think I am, or what you think you're paying me for, but you can take this check and shove it up your exceptionally fine ass!" She grabbed the check from her purse, crumpled it and tossed it at his chest.

The check bounced to the desk and Peyton expected Quinn's expression to give her great satisfaction. Instead, he was staring to her right, worry and anxiety in his eyes.

She turned, startled.

An elderly man sat hunched in a wheelchair in front of the bank of windows overlooking the city. He had thinning white hair and the left side of his face was slack. She spun on her heels, noticing a couple of other men in suits sitting on a leather sofa behind her.

They stared at her as if she were some psychotic lunatic.

Oh, god. What had she done? Her face flamed in mortification. She'd just regressed to the hot-tempered little girl her father had sent away. How had she reverted to such childish behavior? When she'd worked so hard to become a calm, rational person her father would approve of. She should apologize, but…she couldn't make herself say the words.

Her gaze returned to Quinn. He looked pale. Tired. His suit was impeccable, but he had dark circles under his eyes. The island playboy with the easy grin was gone, replaced with this tight-lipped businessman.

A businessman who still smelled of musky sandalwood. Whose very presence caused a burning inside her. A longing for…him.

Quinn cleared his throat and rounded the desk to take the handles of the wheelchair. "If you gentlemen will excuse me, we'll continue this meeting later."

The other men stood, one murmuring, "Of course," and the other grumbled about never finishing the second quarterly report before they shuffled out.

As Quinn pushed the frail old man through the door, Mr. Prescott, Peyton assumed, mumbled something and Quinn bent down to hear him.

Quinn's posture stiffened and he straightened, handing off the wheelchair to his assistant. "I'll talk to you later," he told Prescott.

Quinn turned and stepped back into the room, shutting and locking the door behind him.

The hairs on the back of her neck rose at the look on his face.

He gestured to the sofa. "Have a seat."

Peyton raised her chin and faced him with as much dignity as one could possess in such a situation. Which wasn't much. Couldn't the floor just swallow her up? "This was a mistake. I should go."

"We'll deal with this now." He strode to his desk, leaned his hip on the corner and crossed his arms.

She crossed her arms, as well, irritated at his commanding tone. "There's nothing to deal with. I obviously came at a bad time."

He shrugged. "I have back-to-back meetings the rest of the day."

"Oh, yes, the island playboy who's consumed by work."

He chuckled, shaking his head. "If you only knew."

His condescending smirk drove her past caring. "I know you're a liar and that you like to play cruel jokes."

The smile disappeared and his eyes narrowed. "You don't know me at all."

"Exactly, *Mr. Smith*. If only I'd known the real you this weekend." A lump formed in her throat. She felt ridiculously close to tears.

He shoved off the desk and closed the distance between them. "You want to know the real me? I'm Prescott's bastard. The son he never wanted until he needed me."

Peyton refused to back down. "So you think that gives you the right to play with people's lives?"

"I wasn't playing. Well, I was, but— Not like you think, damn it." Dragging a hand through his hair, he brushed past her.

She turned to see him drop onto the sofa.

"I just needed to get away from this…prison," he continued. "I wanted a couple of days to forget about Prescott Industries." He said the last two words as if they were fungus in a petri dish.

"Why?"

"Because I made a deal with the devil."

Keeping her arms folded, she shifted her weight from one foot to the other, waiting for him to explain.

Quinn sighed and leaned forward, his elbows braced on his knees. "My mother was Prescott's mistress. When she told him she was pregnant, he wanted her to get rid of me. And when she refused, he cut her off without a cent. She did her best to raise me, but by the time I was in high school I was getting stoned and stealing cars."

He dropped his gaze briefly, and then resumed eye contact. "I'd have ended up a felon if she hadn't swallowed her pride and gone to ask for his help. He hired the best lawyer money could buy and got my sentence reduced."

Quinn stood, tugged his blue silk tie loose and stalked around the room like a restless tiger in a cage. "But the only reason he agreed to help me was because he didn't have anyone else. No kids. His wife had died. All he had was his company, but that would've been sold off when he died." Finally stopping at the bank of windows, he stuffed his hands in his slacks pockets and stared outside. "Hence, my freedom came with a price."

After their weekend together, Peyton could picture Quinn as a rebellious delinquent. Yet he also seemed perfectly at ease in his tailor-made suit and his executive offices. And she could see the hurt boy in his eyes when he turned. "But you can bet your exceptionally fine ass I made sure my mother was taken care of for life."

Her chest hurt knowing exactly what it felt like not to be wanted. "So, you became his protégé?"

He huffed. "More like his lackey."

"Still, you seem to have come out on top."

"Oh, I earned a degree. Learned to run the company. And when he said jump, I asked how high, although I never let him forget how much I hated him."

Hairs rose along her arms. So much venom. She could relate. Ever since her father sent her off to boarding school, Peyton had made sure he was well aware of her unhappiness. In choosing to bury her emotions, she'd made sure to be as cold and unfeeling as he was. And she'd succeeded. "And do you hate him still?"

He smiled. "Funny thing about hate. It takes a lot of energy to maintain that kind of anger. One day, a few years ago, my mother wisely told me that my hatred of the old man was like taking poison every day and hoping *he* would die."

Peyton blinked as those words of wisdom sank in. Whoa. Is that what she was doing? Poisoning herself with years of resentment?

She thought about the last time she'd talked to her father, just before she'd gotten on the plane for Rapture Island. Dad had casually suggested she try to come home for Christmas.

At the time, Peyton had chalked the invitation up to a shallow platitude. But as she thought back on it, she let herself hear the sincerity in her dad's voice. The longing for a relationship.

"Powerful stuff, huh?" Quinn spoke from just a couple of feet away. He'd moved closer while she'd been reminiscing. "Makes you think about things. And while you're examining your life, think about this. You weren't exactly a fount of truthfulness when I first met you, Professor Monahan." His gaze roamed down her body. She'd worn her usual professor clothes—long khaki pants, a polo shirt buttoned all the way up and an old corduroy jacket, complete with elbow patches.

"I've done a little checking on you since I got back in town." He fingered the top button of her shirt. "Is this the real you? Or are you the woman who went to bed with a complete stranger?"

She blinked at him, unable to answer. She didn't know.

"Want to know what I think?" He closed the distance between them, encroaching on her personal space. "I think you hide the real Peyton behind these wrinkled clothes and the old lady hairdo. The woman I knew on the island was brave and exciting."

Brave? Exciting? Was that how he saw her? That wasn't the real Peyton. Or was it? She was so confused. All those messy emotions she'd had no trouble ignoring the past twenty-odd years churned inside her, causing her to doubt everything she'd always held as fact.

Suck it up, Monahan. She tried shoving all her feelings back into the box she'd duct-taped closed and labeled Too Much Drama as a teen. Back where they belonged, never to be dealt with again. It was bad enough she'd caused a scene in front of a room full of businesspeople.

"It doesn't matter anymore. We don't have to ever see each other again." She moved around Quinn and grabbed the door handle.

Quinn caught her wrist and twirled her to face him. "This is *so* not over." He backed her against the door, leaning into her. "The truth is I lied about who I was that morning because I wanted more time with you." His lips were inches from hers, his light brown eyes glittering. "If I had told you I represented Prescott Industries, you would have left that day and we'd have never gone parasailing over the Caribbean." He brought a hand up and smoothed a strand of her hair away from her cheek and followed his fingers with his mouth. "Spending that day with you was one of my best days ever."

"It was?" Peyton closed her eyes as his warm breath touched her temple.

He drew back and she opened her eyes to find his gaze on hers. Before she could draw a breath, he was kissing her. Desperate, hungry kisses, angling his head to take her mouth one way, then the other. She was falling, surrendering to the onslaught of his mouth, of his arms holding her tight. Of his words. *He'd wanted more time with her.*

"Peyton," he whispered, pulling her hair loose from its knot. "I sent that damn check hoping it would bring you back to me somehow." He kissed down her jaw. "I had to see you again."

"Why?"

"Over the years, working for the old man, I'd somehow lost myself. Spending time with you, I got a piece of Quinn Smith back. Something about you reminds me to be me."

She shuddered and gave in. She dug her nails into his scalp and kissed him back. In seconds, he'd helped her shed her jacket. He dragged his lips down the hollow of her throat and at the same time wrenched off his suit coat and tie.

He touched his forehead to hers and stilled. "But I also sent that check because, no matter what, I want you to find that cave. The monk and his princess risked their lives to save those Mayan writings, and they deserve to be seen by the world."

Peyton blinked back tears. "That's exactly how I feel."

"I know. *You* made me see that. That Spanish monk was one romantic dude. 'She makes me feel alive and terrified and tender all at once,'" he quoted.

"The monk wrote that." She gasped. "The diary! You have it?"

"You left it in my room. It must have fallen out of your bag."

"You read it?"

He shrugged. "It's a great story."

She shook her head in awe. He'd read the whole diary? How many men would bother to read a four-hundred-year old diary?

"I remembered that line because that's how I feel about you." He kissed the tip of her nose. "Alive—" he kissed her forehead "—and terrified—" then he kissed her temple "—and tender."

"Me, too." The words slipped out before she thought.

Quinn stepped back, his hands cupping her elbows. "You feel that way about me?"

She thought back to their day—and nights—together. How he'd enjoyed life and lived every moment to the fullest. His enthusiasm had been contagious. By comparison, her life seemed dull and routine.

The monk's love for the Mayan woman had completely disrupted his world. They'd had to flee for their lives and start over in a strange city. But their love for each other couldn't be denied.

Peyton had a small circle of friends, but how many weekends could one spend playing Trivial Pursuit? Life with Quinn had been exciting and unexpected. But he was also responsible and caring.

She'd experienced more joy with Quinn this past weekend than ever before in her life. And more pain. Did opening oneself up to emotions always have to be painful? In just these few short moments with Quinn, she'd somehow let go of her anger at her father. Years of pain dissolved.

Maybe that was the secret. To be open to life and tenderness, one had to be open to terror and pain, as well. But it was worth it to feel this kind of…love?

She wrapped her arms around his neck and pulled him close. "I'm terrified, but so alive. I want to take a chance on us. I want to jump off a cliff with you again."

He grinned. "You like living life on the edge?"

She returned his smile. "It's exciting." Some things were worth all the drama and crisis.

Taking a deep breath, he glanced heavenward. "I've created a monster."

"Hey." She pretended to pout. "I was crashing weddings before I ever met you."

"Weddings, offices… That's twice you've crashed into my life, Monahan."

"Hmm, maybe you should send me an engraved invitation next time." Pulling his mouth to hers, she kissed him.

* * * * *

Harlequin *Blaze*

COMING NEXT MONTH

Blaze's 10ᵗʰ Anniversary
Special Collectors' Editions

Available July 26, 2011

#627 THE BRADDOCK BOYS: TRAVIS
Love at First Bite
Kimberly Raye

#628 HOTSHOT
Uniformly Hot!
Jo Leigh

#629 UNDENIABLE PLEASURES
The Pleasure Seekers
Tori Carrington

#630 COWBOYS LIKE US
Sons of Chance
Vicki Lewis Thompson

#631 TOO HOT TO TOUCH
Legendary Lovers
Julie Leto

#632 EXTRA INNINGS
Encounters
Debbi Rawlins

You can find more information on upcoming
Harlequin® titles, free excerpts and more at
www.HarlequinInsideRomance.com.

HBCNM0711

REQUEST YOUR FREE BOOKS!
2 FREE NOVELS PLUS 2 FREE GIFTS!

Harlequin *Blaze*

red-hot reads!

*Once bitten, twice shy. That's Gabby Wade's motto—
especially when it comes to Adamson men.
And the moment she meets Jon Adamson her theory
is confirmed. But with each encounter a little something
sparks between them, making her wonder if she's been
too hasty to dismiss this one!*

*Enjoy this sneak peek from ONE GOOD REASON
by Sarah Mayberry, available August 2011
from Harlequin® Superromance®.*

Gabby Wade's heartbeat thumped in her ears as she marched
to her office. She wanted to pretend it was because of her
brisk pace returning from the file room, but she wasn't that
good a liar.

Her heart was beating like a tom-tom because Jon Adamson had touched her. In a very male, very possessive way.
She could still feel the heat of his big hand burning through
the seat of her khakis as he'd steadied her on the ladder.

It had taken every ounce of self-control to tell him to
unhand her. What she'd really wanted was to grab him by
his shirt and, well, explore all those urges his touch had
instantly brought to life.

While she might not like him, she was wise enough to
understand that it wasn't always about liking the other person. Sometimes it was about pure animal attraction.

Refusing to think about it, she turned to work. When
she'd typed in the wrong figures three times, Gabby admitted she was too tired and too distracted. Time to call it a
day.

As she was leaving, she spied Jon at his workbench in
the shop. His head was propped on his hand as he studied
blueprints. It wasn't until she got closer that she saw his

eyes were shut.

He looked oddly boyish. There was something innocent and unguarded in his expression. She felt a weakening in her resistance to him.

"Jon." She put her hand on his shoulder, intending to shake him awake. Instead, it rested there like a caress.

His eyes snapped open.

"You were asleep."

"No, I was, uh, visualizing something on this design." He gestured to the blueprint in front of him then rubbed his eyes.

That gesture dealt a bigger blow to her resistance. She realized it wasn't only animal attraction pulling them together. She took a step backward as if to get away from the knowledge.

She cleared her throat. "I'm heading off now."

He gave her a smile, and she could see his exhaustion.

"Yeah, I should, too." He stood and stretched. The hem of his T-shirt rose as he arched his back and she caught a flash of hard male belly. She looked away, but it was too late. Her mind had committed the image to permanent memory.

And suddenly she knew, for good or bad, she'd never look at Jon the same way again.

Find out what happens next in ONE GOOD REASON, available August 2011 from Harlequin® Superromance®!

Celebrating

Blaze™
10 *years of*
red-hot reads

Featuring a special August author lineup of
six fan-favorite authors who have written
for Blaze™ from the beginning!

The Original Sexy Six:
Vicki Lewis Thompson
Tori Carrington
Kimberly Raye
Debbi Rawlins
Julie Leto
Jo Leigh

Pick up all six Blaze™
Special Collectors' Edition titles!
August 2011

Plus visit
HarlequinInsideRomance.com
and click on the Series Excitement Tab
for exclusive Blaze™ 10th Anniversary content!

www.Harlequin.com

USA TODAY *bestselling author*

Lynne Graham

introduces her new Epic Duet

THE VOLAKIS VOW

A marriage made of secrets...

Tally Spencer, an ordinary girl with no experience of
relationships... Sander Volakis, an impossibly rich and
handsome Greek entrepreneur. Sander is expecting to
love her and leave her, but for Tally this is love at first
sight. Little does he know that Tally is expecting his
baby...and blackmailing him to marry her!

PART ONE:
THE MARRIAGE BETRAYAL
Available August 2011

PART TWO:
BRIDE FOR REAL
Available September 2011

Available only from Harlequin Presents®.